CINDERELLA AND
THE BILLIONAIRE

CINDERELLA AND THE BILLIONAIRE

MARION LENNOX

MILLS & BOON

First published in Great Britain 2019
by Mills & Boon, an imprint of HarperCollins*Publishers*
1 London Bridge Street, London, SE1 9GF

Large Print edition 2019

© 2019 Marion Lennox

ISBN: 978-0-263-08299-9

Printed and bound in Great Britain
by CPI Group (UK) Ltd, Croydon, CR0 4YY

To our friends, Neil and Dale,
and to all the intrepid islanders who
make their homes and/or their livings
on the islands of Bass Strait.

It's a harsh and unforgiving place
to love, but it gives back in spades.

PROLOGUE

THE LACEWORK ON McLellan Place's gatehouse looked almost perfect. From the helicopter, Matt and Henry saw the last piece being fitted into place. Once they landed they admired the result, agreeing with the foreman that it had been a major storm. The damage wasn't the fault of workmanship.

If Matt had come by himself he might have headed straight back to Manhattan, but he was entertaining a seven-year-old. He and Henry therefore walked across the vast sweep of lawn to the main house beyond.

'It's big,' Henry whispered as Matt led him into the massive kitchen and through to the butler's pantry to find juice and cookies. The place was always stocked, even though Matt was lucky to arrive once a month.

The house *was* big, Matt conceded. With eight bathrooms and ten bedrooms, it was far too large for one semireclusive bachelor. But the

East Hampton home, two hours' drive or a short chopper ride from Manhattan, had been in his family for generations. Its upkeep kept a team of locals employed, its seclusion gave wildlife a precious refuge and it was as much a home as he'd ever known. It had been his refuge as a child from being dragged from one international hotel to another by his jet-setting parents.

Henry should have somewhere like this, he thought. McLellan Place was a far cry from the Manhattan legal offices where Henry seemed to spend half his life.

The seven-year-old was now sitting at the vast stretch of granite that formed the kitchen bench, seriously concentrating on his juice. He was nothing to do with Matt, but there was a part of Matt that connected with him.

Henry's mother, Amanda, was one of Matt's employees, a lawyer and a good one. Nothing got in the way of her work, including her son. When he wasn't at school she left him in her office and often, somehow, he ended up in Matt's office, reading or playing computer games.

The call today, to tell Matt of the storm damage, had come through when he'd had an unexpected break in appointments. Matt hadn't been near McLellan Place for weeks. His chopper was available. It was time he checked on the place.

He'd looked at the silent kid and made a decision. A call to Amanda had given slightly stunned permission—she couldn't believe her boss had time for the boy.

Thus Henry was here with him, quiet and serious.

'It has beautiful furniture,' the little boy ventured.

It did. His mother's interior designer would be pleased.

'Those stairs are really long.'

'When I was your age I used to slide down the bannisters.' The bannisters were an ode to craftsmanship, the oak curving gracefully at the end to stop a small boy coming to grief. 'Would you like me to show you how?'

'No, thank you.'

Probably just as well. He hadn't slid down for maybe twenty years.

'We have time for a swim,' he suggested. The horizon pool by the house was kept warm all year round.

'I didn't bring my swimmers.'

'We could swim in our jocks.'

'No, thank you,' Henry said again, politely,

and Matt felt like banging his head. This kid had been schooled to be seen and not heard, to fade into the background.

'Then let's go for a walk on the beach,' he told Henry.

And then his personal phone rang. Uh-oh.

Matt's secretary knew what he was doing and when he'd be back. She'd only contact him if it was urgent.

'Helen?'

'Matt?' And by the tone of her voice he knew something was wrong. Seriously wrong.

What the...? 'Tell me.'

'Matt, it's Amanda. You know...she went out to lunch. Matt, they say she was texting and she walked... Matt, she walked straight into traffic. Matt, she's dead. That poor little boy. Oh, Matt, how are you going to tell him?'

CHAPTER ONE

'YOU EMPLOYED ME to act as a fishing guide. Now you want me to act as a glorified taxi driver? *And in* Bertha? Four hours out and four hours back, with overnight stays? Is she even safe?'

'She's safe as houses.' Charlie's voice was smooth as silk as he patted the reservation book with satisfaction. 'This is a last-minute booking, *Bertha*'s the only boat available and Jeff's rung in sick. Have you any idea how much this guy's prepared to pay? Never mind,' he added hastily, no doubt figuring Meg would up her wage demands if she knew. 'But it's enough to give you a decent bonus.'

'Charlie, I've been out since dawn on a fishing charter. I'm filthy. I'm off for the next three days. I have five acres of grass to slash and it's almost fire season. If I don't get it done now the council will be down on me like a ton of bricks.'

'Sell that place and move into town,' Charlie

said easily. 'I know it was your grandpa's, but sentimentality gets you nowhere. Look,' he said placatingly. 'You do this job, and I'll send Graham out to slash the place for you.'

Charlie's son. Not in a million years.

'You're kidding. Knowing Graham, he'd slash the house before he touched the grass. Charlie, I'm not about to drop everything and spend the next three days ferrying some cashed-up tourist with more money than sense. Why does he want to go to Garnett Island anyway? No one goes there.'

'I do.'

The voice made her jump.

She'd been leaning over the counter of Rowan Bay's only charter boat company, focusing on Charlie. Not that Charlie was anything to focus on. He was flabby, florid, and he smelled of fish.

The guy who'd walked in was hitting six feet, maybe even more, lean, ripped, tanned. Sleek? The word seemed to fit. In the circles Meg O'Hara moved in, this guy was...well, a fish out of water.

Or a shark? His smart chinos, his butter-soft leather jacket, his brogues all screamed money. His hair looked as if it had been cut yesterday, conservative and classy, every jet-black wave knowing its place.

And his eyes…

Dark as deep water, they were watching her and asking questions. She found herself getting flustered just looking into those eyes.

'I'm Matt McLellan,' he said softly, but there was a growl underneath, an inherent threat. Was it…*don't mess with me*? 'You're booked to take me to Garnett Island. Is there a problem?'

Charlie stood up so fast his chair fell over behind him. He grabbed a grubby notepad from beside the phone, wrote a figure on it and shoved it across the desk at Meg.

She glanced down at it and turned bug-eyed.

'That'd be my cut?' she asked incredulously. What had this guy offered Charlie?

'Yes,' he said hurriedly and surged around the desk to take the stranger's hand. 'There's no problem, Mr. McLellan. This is Meg O'Hara, your skipper. She'll take you out, anchor until you have the little one settled and then bring you back.'

'Little one?' Meg asked.

'He's taking a boy out to his grandmother,' Charlie said, talking too fast. 'That's right, isn't it, sir?'

'That's right.' The man dropped Charlie's hand and glanced at his own. She saw an almost-instinctive urge to wipe it.

She didn't blame him. Charlie's hands... Ugh.

Though she glanced down at herself and thought... *I'm almost as bad.*

'But you have reservations?' he said. He'd obviously overheard. 'The boat?'

'We had the boat in dry dock just last week,' Charlie said. 'I checked her personally. And Meg here is one of our most experienced skippers. Ten years of commercial fishing and another two years taking fishing charters. There's nothing about the sea she doesn't know.'

'She doesn't look old enough to have done any of those things.'

'Is that a compliment or what?' It was time she was part of this conversation, Meg decided. She knew she looked young, and her jeans, baggy windcheater, short copper curls and no make-up wouldn't be helping. 'I'm twenty-eight. I started fishing with my grandfather when I was sixteen. He got sick when I was twenty-five so we sold the boat and I took a part-time job helping Charlie with fishing charters. My granddad died six months ago, so I can now take longer charters.' She glanced at the note Charlie had given her. This amount… She could even get the leak over the washhouse fixed. 'The boy… Is he your son?'

'I don't have a son.'

Hmm. If she was going to be forthcoming, so was he.

'I'm not about to let you take a kid I know nothing about and dump him on Garnett Island.' She planted her feet square and met him eye to eye. 'Garnett Island's four hours off the mainland. As far as I know, Peggy Lakey lives there and no one else.'

'Peggy's Henry's grandmother.'

'Really?' Local lore said Peggy had no relatives at all. 'How old's Henry?'

'Seven.'

'He's going on a holiday?'

'To stay.'

'Is that right? Are you his legal guardian?'

'It's none of your business.'

'If you want my help it's very much my business.' Behind her she could see Charlie almost weep. The figure he'd scrawled represented a month's takings and that was only her cut. But she had to ignore the money. This was a kid. 'You're American, right?'

'Right.'

'Henry's American, too?'

'Yes.'

'Then you must have had documentation allowing you to bring him out of the country. Giving you authority. Can I see?'

'Meg!' Charlie was almost wringing his hands but Charlie wasn't the one being asked to leave a child on an almost-deserted island.

'You can see,' he said and flipped a wad of documents from an inside pocket and laid them on the desk. Then he glanced outside, as if checking. For the child?

'Where's Henry now?' she asked.

'We just had fish and chips. He's feeding the leftovers to the seagulls.'

'Greasy food before heading to sea? Does he get seasick?'

That brought a frown. 'I didn't think…'

She was flipping through the documents. 'These say you're not even related.'

'I'm not related,' he said and then obviously decided the easiest way to get past her belligerence was to be forthcoming.

'I'm a lawyer and financial analyst in Manhattan,' he said. 'Henry's mother, Amanda, is… *was*…a lawyer in my company. She was a single mother and no one's ever been told who Henry's father is. Henry's quiet. When he's not in school he sits in her office or out in the reception area. He reads or watches his notepad. Then two weeks ago, Amanda was killed. She was on her phone, she walked into traffic and suddenly there was no one for Henry.'

'Oh...' And her head switched from distrust to distress, just like that. Her own parents... A car crash. She'd been eleven.

Her grandparents had been with her from the moment she'd woken in the hospital. She had a sudden vision of a seven-year-old who sat in a reception area and read.

There was no one for Henry.

But she wasn't paid to be emotional. She was paid to get the job done.

'So...your relationship with him?' She was leafing through the documents, trying to get a grip.

'I'm no relation.' His voice was suddenly bleak. 'Sometimes he sits in my office while I work. It was term break, so he was with me when we heard of his mother's death. The birth certificate names the father as Steven Walker but gives no details. We haven't been able to track him down and no one else seems to care. Apart from Peggy.'

And just like that, her bristles turned to fluff.

'Garnett Island?' she said, hauling herself—with difficulty—away from the image she was starting to have of a bereft seven-year-old sitting in a lawyer's office when someone came to tell him his mum was dead.

'As far as we can find out, Peggy Lakey's now Henry's only living relative,' he told her. 'Peggy's his maternal grandmother. Unless we can find his father, she has full say in his upbringing.'

'So why didn't she get straight on a plane?' The solitude of Henry was still all around her.

'She says she turns into a whimpering heap at the sight of a plane. I've talked to her via her radio set-up. She sounds sensible, but flying's not an option. She made arrangements for an escort service to collect Henry and bring him to her, but, at the last minute, I…'

'You couldn't let him travel alone.'

The last of her bristles disintegrated. For some stupid reason she felt her eyes fill. She swiped a hand across her cheek—and felt an oil streak land where the tear had been. Good one, Meg.

'So is that enough?' Matt McLellan's tone turned acerbic, moving on. 'Can we leave?'

'After I've double-checked *Bertha*,' she told

him with a sideways glance at Charlie. He'd checked her personally? Yeah, and she was a monkey's uncle. She could at least give the engine a quick once-over. 'And when you and Henry have taken seasickness tablets and let them settle. Bass Strait, Mr McLellan, is not for pussies.'

What was he doing here?

The Cartland case was nearing closure. He had to trust his staff not to mess things up.

He checked his phone and almost groaned. No reception.

'There's not a lot of connectivity in the Southern Ocean.' The skipper—if you could call this slip of a kid a skipper—was being helpful. 'You can use the radio if it's urgent.'

He'd heard her on the radio. It was a static-filled jumble. Besides, the boat was lurching. A lot.

The boat he was on was a rusty thirty-foot tub. 'She's all that's available,' Charlie had told him. 'You want any better, you'll have to wait until Monday.'

He needed to be back in New York by Monday, so he was stuck.

At least his instinct to distrust everyone in this

tinpot hire company hadn't gone so far as to refuse the pills Meg had insisted on. For which he was now incredibly grateful. His arm was around Henry, holding him close. Henry was almost deathly silent, completely withdrawn, but at least he wasn't throwing up.

They were almost an hour out of Rowan Bay. Three hours to go before they reached Garnett Island.

He thought, not for the first time, how much better a helicopter would have been.

There'd been no helicopters. Apparently there were bush fires inland. Any available chopper had been diverted to firefighting or surveillance, and the ones remaining had been booked up well before he'd decided to come.

Beside him, Henry whimpered and huddled closer. There had been no choice. The thought of sending him here with an unknown travel escort had left him cold.

Dumping him on an isolated island left him cold.

He had no choice.

'Boof!'

He glanced up. Meg had turned to look at Henry, but she was calling her dog?

They'd met Boof as they'd boarded. He was a

rangy red-brown springer spaniel, turning grey in the dignified way of elderly dogs. He'd given them a courteous dog greeting as they'd boarded but Henry had cringed. Taking the hint, the dog had headed to the bow and acted like the carvings Matt had seen on ancient boats in the movies. Nose to the wind, ears flying, he looked fantastic.

Now…one word from Meg and he was by her side.

Meg was fishing deep in the pocket of what looked a truly disgusting oilskin jacket. She produced a plastic packet. Then she lashed the wheel and came over and knelt before Henry.

'Henry,' she said.

Henry didn't respond. Matt felt his little body shake, and with that came the familiar surge of anger on the child's behalf.

In anyone's books, Amanda had been an appalling mother.

Henry had been lonely when Amanda was alive and he was even more alone now.

Meg had obviously decided to join the list of those who felt sorry for the little boy. Now she knelt with her dog beside her, her bag in her hand, and she waited.

'Henry?' she said again.

There was a muffled sniff. There'd been a lot of those lately. Matt's hold on him tightened and slowly the kid's face emerged.

They were both wearing sou'westers Meg had given them. Henry's wan face emerging from a sea of yellow made Matt's heart lurch. He was helpless with this kid. He had no rights at all and now he was taking him…who knew where?

'Henry, Boof hasn't had dinner,' Meg said and waited.

The lashed wheel was doing its job. They were heading into the wind. The boat's action had settled a little.

The sea was all around them. They seemed cocooned, an island of humanity and dog in the middle of nowhere.

'Boof needs to be fed,' Meg said, as if it didn't matter too much. 'He loves being fed one doggy bit at a time, and I have to go back to the wheel. Do you think you could feed Boof for me?'

There was an almost-imperceptible shake of the head.

Unperturbed, Meg opened the packet. 'I guess I can do the first bit. Boof, sit.'

Boof sat right before her.

'Ask,' Meg said.

Boof dropped to the deck, looked imploringly

up at Meg, then went back to sitting. He raised a paw. *Please?*

Matt almost laughed.

That was saying something. There hadn't been any laughter in the last two weeks.

But Meg's face was solemn. 'Great job, Boof,' she told him and offered one doggy bit. Boof appeared to consider, then delicately accepted.

And Henry was transfixed.

'Does he do that all the time?' he whispered.

'His table manners are perfect,' Meg said, giving Boof a hug. 'Boof, would you like another one? Ask.'

The performance was repeated, with the addition of a sweep of wagging tail. This was obviously a performance Boof enjoyed.

There were quite a few doggy bits.

But Meg glanced back at the wheel. 'Boof, sorry, you'll have to wait.' She headed back to the wheel, and Boof dropped to the deck, dejection in every fibre of his being.

'Can't you give him the rest?' Henry ventured, and Matt could have cheered.

'If I have time later.' Meg's attention was back on the ocean.

And Matt could feel Henry's tension.

From the time he'd heard of his mother's death,

he'd been almost rigid. With shock? Fear? Who knew? He'd accepted the news without a word.

Social Services had been there early. Talking to Matt. *If there's no one, we'll take care of him until we can contact his grandmother.*

Matt hardly had the time or the skills to care for a child, but in the face of Henry's stoic acceptance his voice had seemed to come from nowhere.

I'll take care of him, he'd said.

Almost immediately he'd thought, *What have I done?*

To say Matt McLellan wasn't a family man was to put it mildly. He'd been an only child with distant parents. He'd had a few longer-term lovers, but they'd been women who followed his rules. Career and independence came first.

Matt had been raised pretty much the same as Henry. Care had been paid for by money. But he hadn't been deserted when he was seven. His almost-visceral reaction to Henry's loss had shocked him.

So Henry had come home to Matt's apartment. The place had great views overlooking the Hudson. It had the best that money could buy when it came to furnishings and art, but Matt pretty much used it as a place to crash. In terms of comfort for a seven-year-old there was nothing.

They'd gone back to Amanda's apartment to fetch what Henry needed and found almost a carbon copy of Matt's place. The apartment was spotless. Henry's room had designer children's prints on the walls but it still spoke sterile. His toys were arranged almost as if they were supposed to be part of the artwork.

Henry had taken a battered teddy and a scrapbook that Matt had had the privilege to see.

He'd wanted nothing else.

The scrapbook was in his backpack now. There was panic when it was out of reach, so the backpack had pretty much stayed on for the entire trip. And Teddy… When Matt had put on his oversized sou'wester, Henry had tucked Teddy deep in the pocket, almost as if he expected someone to snatch it away.

A kid. A scrapbook. A teddy.

There'd been nothing else. And Matt had had no idea how to comfort him.

'Maybe we could feed the dog,' Matt said and waited some more.

'Boof likes boys more than grown-ups,' Meg said from the wheel. 'Though he likes me best.

The same as your teddy, Henry. I bet your teddy likes you best.'

So she'd seen. His respect for her went up a notch.

Actually, his respect was mounting.

Even though it had annoyed him at the time, he'd accepted—even appreciated—her checking his authority to take Henry to the island. And her skill now... The way she turned the boat to the wind, her concentration on each swell... They combined to provide the most comfortable and safe passage possible.

She was small and thin. Her copper curls looked as if they'd been attacked by scissors rather than a decent hairdresser. She'd ditched her oilskin and was now wearing faded jeans and a windcheater with the words *Here, Fishy* on the back. Her feet were bare and she seemed totally oblivious to the wind.

Her tanned face, her crinkled eyes... This woman was about as far from the women he mixed with as it was possible to get.

And now she was focused on Henry. He saw Henry's surprise as Meg mentioned Teddy. Henry's hand slipped into his pocket as if he was reassuring himself that Ted was still there.

'Ted likes me.'

'Of course,' Meg agreed. 'Like Boof likes me. But Boof does love friends giving him his dinner.'

She went back to concentrating on the wheel. Boof sat beside her but looked back at Henry. As if he knew what was expected of him. As if he knew how to draw a scared child into his orbit.

Had there been kids in the past, scared kids on this woman's fishing charters? He couldn't fault the performance.

But there was no pressure. Maybe it was only Matt who was holding his breath.

Boof walked back over to Henry, gazed into his face, gave a gentle whine and raised a paw. Matt glanced up at Meg and saw the faintest of smiles.

Yep, this was a class act, specifically geared to draw a sucker in. And Henry was that sucker and Matt wasn't complaining one bit.

'Can I have the doggy bits?' Henry quavered.

Meg said, 'Sure,' and tossed the bag. Matt caught it but she'd already turned back to the wheel.

No pressure…

He could have kissed her.

He needed to follow Meg's lead. He dropped the bag on Henry's knee. 'You might get your fingers dirty,' he said, as if he almost disapproved of what Henry might do.

'I can wipe them,' Henry said.

'I guess.'

Henry nodded. Cautiously, he opened the bag.

'Sit,' he said to Boof, and Boof, who'd stood with alacrity the moment the bag opened, sat.

'Ask,' Henry said and the plan went swimmingly. A doggy bit went down the hatch. Boof's tail waved and then he raised a paw again. His plea was obvious. Repeat.

It was such a minor act, but for Matt, who'd cared for an apathetic bundle of misery for two weeks without knowing how to break through, it felt like gold. He glanced up at Meg, expecting her to be still focusing on the sea, but she wasn't. Her smile was almost as wide as his.

Did she know how important this was? She'd seen the legal documents. He'd told her the gist of the tragedy.

Her smile met his. He mouthed a silent thank you with his smile, and her smile said, *You're welcome.*

And that smile…

Back at the boatshed she'd said she was twenty-eight. He'd hardy believed her, but now, seeing the depth of understanding behind her smile...

It held maturity, compassion and understanding. And it made him feel...

That was hardly appropriate.

She turned back to the wheel and his gaze dropped to her feet. The soles were stained and the skin was cracked.

She'd said she'd been fishing since she was sixteen. She was so far out of his range of experience she might as well have come from another planet. There was no reason—and no way—he could even consider getting to know her better. That flash of...whatever it was...was weird.

He went back to watching Henry feed Boof, one doggy bit at a time. The little boy was relaxing with every wag of the dog's tail. Finally the bits were gone. He expected Meg to call Boof back, or that the dog would resume his stance at the bow. Instead, the dog leaped onto the seat beside Henry and laid his big, boofy head on Henry's lap.

Matt glanced up at Meg and, surprised, saw the end of a doggy command—the gesture of clicked fingers.

Part of the service?

She grinned at him and winked. *Winked?*

Henry was feeling Boof's soft ears. He wiggled his fingers, and the dog rolled his head, almost in ecstasy.

Henry giggled.

Not such a big thing?

Huge.

His hold on him tightened. This kid was the child of a business connection. Nothing more, but that giggle almost did him in.

He glanced back at Meg and found her watching him. Him. Not Henry. His face. Seeing his reaction.

For some reason that made him feel... exposed?

That was nuts. He was here to deliver a child to his grandmother and move on. There was no need for emotion.

He didn't do emotion. He hardly knew how. That Meg had somehow made Henry smile, that she'd figured how to make him feel secure... How did she know how to do it?

Matt McLellan was a man in charge of his world. He knew how to keep it ordered, but for some reason this woman was making him feel as if there was a world out there he knew nothing about.

And when Henry snuggled even closer, when Henry's hands stilled on the big dog's head, when Henry's eyes fluttered closed… When he fell asleep against Matt with all the trust in the world, the feeling intensified.

Once again he glanced at Meg and found her watching. And the way she looked at him…

It was as if she saw all the way through and out the other side.

She shouldn't be here. She should be home, slashing her grass, doing something about Grandpa's veggie patch. If he could see the mess it was in, he'd turn in his grave. That veggie patch had been his pride and joy.

She'd let it run down. She'd had no choice. The last months of her grandfather's life he'd been almost totally dependent. She didn't begrudge it one bit but she'd come out the other side deep in debt. She now had to take every fishing charter she could get.

The veggie patch was almost mocking her.

She should sell the whole place and move on. It'd cover her debts. She could go north, get a job in a charter company that wasn't as dodgy as Charlie's, make herself a new life.

Except the house was all she had left of Grandpa. All she had left of her parents.

Stop it. There was nothing she could do to solve her problems now, so there was no use thinking about them. She was heading out to Garnett Island. The money would help. That was all that mattered.

Except, as the hours wore on, as *Bertha* shovelled her way inexorably through the waves, she found herself inexplicably drawn to the man and child seated in the stern.

They'd exchanged niceties when they'd first boarded: the weather, her spiel about the history of this coast, the dolphins, the birds they might see. The guy… Matt…had asked a few desultory questions. Other than that, they'd hardly talked. The child had seemed bereft and the guy seemed as if he didn't want to be here.

And then she'd convinced Henry to feed Boof and something had happened. She'd seen them both change. She'd seen the kid light up. She'd seen him pat Boof and then snuggle into the side of the man beside him.

And she'd seen Matt look as if he was about to cry.

What was it between the pair of them? What

was a Manhattan financier doing carting a kid down into the Southern Ocean to dump him on Garnett Island?

Except the guy now looked as if he'd cracked wide open. He cared. Something had shifted inside him, and when he'd smiled at her...

Um...not. Let's not go there. This was a seriously good-looking guy being nice to an orphan, and if that wasn't a cliché for hearts and violins nothing was.

But that smile...

Was nothing to do with her. She was doing a job, nothing else.

They were getting close to Garnett now. She could see its bulk in the distance. There were a couple of uninhabited rocky outcrops in between, the result of some long-ago volcanic disturbance. She needed to watch her charts, watch the depth sounder. Not think about the pair behind her.

And then, suddenly, she had something else to think about. *Bertha* coughed.

Or that was what it sounded like, and after a lifetime spent at sea Meg was nuanced to every changing engine sound. She checked the dials.

Heat?

What the...? She'd checked everything obvious. How could the engine be heating? And almost as she thought it, she caught her first faint whiff.

Smoke.

CHAPTER TWO

SMOKE?

Oh, dear God.

Meg had a sudden flashback to a couple of days back. She'd been bringing in a fishing charter and she'd seen Graham, Charlie's son, coming out of the inlet. He'd been in this boat.

Rowan Bay was a marine reserve, a fish breeding ground. It was tidal, shallow, full of drifting sand and water grasses. It was a good place to add to your catch for the day—if you weren't caught by the fisheries officers.

And if you didn't care about your boat.

She was suddenly hearing her grandpa's voice.

You go in there in anything bigger than a dinghy, you're an idiot. Operating in murky waters can cause blockages in the cooling-water intake. That can lead to engine overheating.

Graham was an idiot.

But now wasn't the time for blaming. Almost

instinctively, she shut the motor down, grabbed the fire extinguisher and headed below.

The whiff of smoke became a wall.

Meg O'Hara was not known to panic. There'd been dramas at sea before. She'd swum to shore when a motor died. She'd dived overboard to clear a fouled propeller. She'd even coped with a punter having a heart attack as he'd caught a truly excellent bluefin tuna.

But fire at sea, this far out…

Fire extinguishers had limited volume. It was useless to simply point it at smoke and pull the trigger. But how to get to the seat of the fire?

She hauled her windcheater over her face and tried to open the hatch over the engine…

Flames.

'Get out.' The voice was harsh, deep, and then repeated, a roar of command. She hesitated, shoving the extinguisher forward, trying desperately to see…

'Now!' And a hand hooked the collar of her windcheater and hauled her upward.

She dropped the extinguisher and went. He was right. The speed of this fire…

There was a bag at the entrance to the galley. Heavy. Lifesaving. She grabbed it and lugged it upward.

'Let it go,' the voice roared, and the hand on her collar was insistent.

Pigs might fly, she thought, clinging like a limpet as the hand hauled her higher. And then she was out on the deck, clinging to her precious bag.

'The tender...' A condition of charters in these waters was that a lifeboat was with them at all times and she'd checked the inflatable dinghy before she left. Thank God. The deck was now a cloud of smoke. If the fuel went...

She had to get the tender into the water and get them all into it. Now!

She grabbed the lifeboat's stern pulley. Matt was beside her, seeing what she was doing, matching her at the bow. Lowering it with her.

It hit the water. Almost before it did, she grabbed Henry and thrust him into Matt's arms.

'In. Now.' She grabbed one of the lines from the tender and thrust it into his hand. 'Don't let go. If you fall in, shove the tender away from the boat and pull yourselves in.'

'You take him,' Matt snapped.

'Don't be a fool.' The engine could go up at any minute. 'Take care of the kid. Go.'

She copped a flash of concern but the decision was made. Henry had to be his first priority. He lifted the stunned Henry onto the side of the boat, steadied for a moment and slipped downward.

Thank God she had them both in lifejackets. Getting into an inflatable from a wallowing boat was fraught at the best of times. But he had Henry in, tucking him into the bow. Then he was standing, holding on to the boat. 'You!'

It was the kind of order her grandfather would have made. A no-nonsense order, the kind you didn't mess with, but she still had stuff to do.

'Boof!' she yelled and the big dog was in her arms. She thrust him downward and somehow Matt caught him.

'Get down here,' he yelled.

She could no longer see him. The smoke was all around her.

One last thing…

She grabbed her bag and slid over the side. Strong hands caught her, steadied, but she allowed herself a mere half a second for that steadying. Then she was at the tiller of the tender. The little engine purred into life. *Thank You, God.*

Without being asked, Matt was shoving with all his might, pushing the tender as far from the boat as he could.

Into gear... Full power... Away.

And maybe twenty seconds later the fuel tank caught and *Bertha* erupted into a ball of flames.

She kept the tender at full throttle. The danger wasn't passed yet. Burning fuel could spread across water.

A minute. Two. The distance between them and the flames was growing. She could breathe again.

Just.

She did a quick head count. Not that it was necessary but she needed it for her sanity.

Matt. Henry. Boof. Bag.

They should survive.

'Wow, that was exciting. We're safe now, though, Henry. We're okay.'

He couldn't think what else to say. Matt sat in the bow of the little boat and held Henry. Tight. He was giving comfort, he told himself, but the feel of the child against him, the solidness of the little body, *the safeness of him...* It was a two-way street.

The charter boat was now a smouldering wreck. The flames were dying. It was already starting to look skeletal.

They'd been so lucky. From the time he'd seen

Meg's head jerk around, heard her cut the engine, from the time he'd caught the first whiff of smoke himself... A minute? It must have been more but it didn't feel like it.

He felt stunned to numbness.

They were safe.

Meg was at the tiller. She was coughing, but she was in control. She'd been hit by a wall of smoke as she'd gone below and she'd fought him for that stupid bag. When she'd got herself together, he was going to have words with her about that bag. Like passengers on an airliner trying to save their carry-ons after a crash landing, she could have killed them all. His and Henry's baggage was now ashes, and he wasn't grieving about it one bit. For her to fight to get her bag...

Mind, there was nothing unprofessional about the rest of the way she'd performed. She'd moved seamlessly. All he'd done was follow what she was doing. She'd made them safe.

Safe was a good word. A great word.

He held Henry and let it sink in.

And then he thought, Where are we?

Maybe they weren't so safe.

Meg had pointed out Garnett Island to him a few moments ago. It was still in the distance, surely too far to head for in these seas, in this little boat. The tender was sitting low already. The swells didn't cause a problem but the wind was causing a chop on the top of the water. Meg was steering into the wind, minimising water resistance, but if one of those waves veered sideways...

He looked ahead and saw where she was steering.

A rocky outcrop rose, almost like a sentinel, straight up from the ocean floor. Maybe half a kilometre from them? Maybe less. It looked rough and inhospitable, but part of the rock face seemed to have slipped, forming what seemed a little bay. A few hardy plants must have fought their way to survival, because there was a tinge of green.

'That's where we'll land,' Meg said, watching his look, and then she had to stop and cough again. And again.

She buckled, fighting for breath. She'd copped so much smoke.

'We're swapping places,' he said.

'I'm not moving anywhere.' Every word was a gasp.

Time to be brutal.

'No choice. Your breathing's compromised.

Think about what happens if you collapse at the tiller.'

'You can't…'

'I can handle a boat.'

And he saw her shoulders sag, just a little. Relief? She was only just holding herself together, he thought, and with that thought came another. She'd gone down below, to try to fight a burning engine.

'The flames… Is your throat burned?'

'Only…only smoke. Not…burned.'

'Good, but you're still moving. When I say go, move.'

She didn't reply, fighting another paroxysm of coughing.

'Meg needs help,' he told Henry. He was torn. Henry needed to be held, but the tiller had to be priority.

Boof was on the floor of the boat, crouched low, almost as if he knew stability was an issue. He took Henry's hand and guided it down to the dog's collar. 'I want you to hold on to Boof,' he told him. 'He'll be worried. Hold him tight. Don't let him move, will you?'

And to his relief he got a silent nod in response. Excellent. Not only would Henry's hold anchor him to the big dog, it'd keep him low, as well.

Right. Meg. The tiller.

He watched the sea, waiting for his chance. The next swell swept by. No chop.

Now.

One minute she was holding the tiller, trying to stop the coughs racking her body, trying to keep control. The next…

Matt seemed to come from nowhere. Keeping his body low, he was suddenly at her end of the boat, though with enough sense to keep his weight back as far as he could. Crouching low, he tugged her hard against him, pulling her forward. For one long moment he held her still, checking balance, checking the waves.

Another swell passed—and then she was swung around and propelled onto the central seat.

And then Matt had the tiller and she was no longer in control.

His hold had been swift, firm to the point of brutal, a hard, strong grasp that had left her with nowhere to go. In any other circumstance it would have been terrifying, but right now she'd needed it. It was the assurance that responsibility wasn't all hers. That she wasn't alone.

It was a feeling that made her almost light-headed.

Though maybe that was the smoke.

She was still struggling to breathe. Matt might be in control, he might have reassured her that the boat was being cared for, but she needed air.

Smoke inhalation…

She'd done first-aid training. Grandpa had insisted and he'd also insisted on her updating over and over.

'The bag…' she managed and then subsided again. Oh, her chest hurt.

Matt was handling the tiller, watching the sea, but in between she could see him coming to grips with controls. He was also watching Henry, but he flashed her a glance that told her he was almost as worried as she was about her lungs.

He looked down at the bag. She'd seen his reaction as she'd tossed it down to him—*what, you're worried about luggage?* Now, though… He wasn't a fool. He had the bag opened in seconds, and, still with one eye on the oncoming sea, he started checking the contents.

The first-aid kit lay on top.

What she needed apart from a canister of oxygen—which she didn't have—was a bronchodilator. Albuterol. It was in the first-aid kit to cope with possible asthma attacks.

'Alb…alb…' she gasped but he got it. He had the small canister clear, and she clutched it as if she were drowning.

'You know how to use it?'

She did. She'd used it once on an overweight fisherman with a scary wheeze. She held it and inhaled, held it and inhaled.

Matt was steadied the little boat and turned her slightly away from the outcrop they were heading for, making a sensible adjustment to their path so it was more of a zigzag. It would stop the sideways swell.

He knew boats, then.

Maybe panic had as much to do with the coughing as smoke did, she thought. As she felt her breathing ease…as she watched Matt turn the tiller to avoid a cresting chop…as she twisted in the boat and saw Henry, crouched over Boof, holding his collar and even speaking reassuringly to him…her world seemed to settle.

For now they were safe. Moving on.

They needed help.

Radio…

'There's a radio in the bag, too,' she managed. The coughing wasn't over but at least she could talk. 'And a GPS tracker. In the side pocket.' She subsided and coughed a bit more while she watched Matt delve into the bag again.

And come up with nothing.

'There's nothing in the side pocket.'

'There must be.'

No charter boat went to sea without an emergency radio and tracker beacon. It was illegal to leave port without them. Every boat in Charlie's Marine Services therefore held a bag such as the one Meg had rescued. The presence of the bag was one of the things she checked, every time she boarded. She hadn't checked the contents today, though. There'd been no need. The contents were standard, always in there.

But *Bertha* wasn't usually used for charters.

No!

'What?' Matt went back to looking at the sea but she could tell by the rigidity of his shoulders that he'd sensed something was wrong. Seriously wrong.

'My idiot boss.' She buckled and coughed a bit more, and maybe that was caused by panic, as well. She was trying to make herself think.

Radios and GPS trackers had batteries that ran

out. Charlie ran a regular schedule of checking, because it was sensible, but also, if any marine inspector found a charter boat without a working GPS beacon, or a radio with a flat battery, he'd be down on them like a ton of bricks.

But if such an inspector had come…say, last week…and Charlie had panicked and realised one of the sets was flat…

Why not grab the set from *Bertha*'s bag? *Bertha* wasn't being used for charters. She wouldn't be checked.

All these things were flying through her head like shrapnel. Her head felt as if it might explode. For one awful moment she thought she might be sick.

And then Matt's hand was on her head. He was leaning forward, propelling her downward.

'Head between your knees until it passes,' he said. 'And there's no need to panic. We're safe. One step at a time, Meg.'

She had no choice but to obey. She ducked her head and started counting breaths. It was a trick her grandpa had taught her after her parents had been killed.

When all else fails, just feel your breath on your lips, lass. That's all that matters. One breath after another.

It felt wimpy. It felt as if she'd handed total responsibility to a stranger but she put her head down and counted.

She was up to about a hundred and twenty before she heard Henry, his thin little voice piping up from the back. 'Where are we going?'

She should answer. She should...

'We're going over to that big rock you see in front of you.' And Matt sounded totally in control, as if he were stranded at sea after fire every day of his life.

'Is that Grandma's island?'

'Nope.' Matt's voice sounded almost cheerful. 'We're going to this island first. Garnett Island's a bit far away for us to get there in this little boat.'

'But how will we get to Grandma's?'

Good question, Meg thought. Right now she didn't have an answer. Luckily Matt did.

'We might have to wait awhile,' he conceded. 'But I've been checking this interesting bag our skipper's brought with us. Apart from muesli bars and bags of nuts and sultanas, there are some cool things that look like flares. When you light flares you can be seen for miles. So my guess is that we'll land on this island, we'll eat our muesli bars and our sultanas, and we'll wait for Meg's boss to realise she's no longer in radio contact. I imagine they'll send a helicopter to find us. If we need to, we'll light our flares to help him find us and then we'll all be rescued. Even Boof. Is that a good plan?'

'We might need a drink,' Henry said cautiously.

'There's a water carton under the seat you're sitting on,' Meg managed and then turned and checked herself. All the tenders carried fresh water. At least that was there.

'And what if it gets dark?' Henry quavered.

'I'd imagine Meg's boss will send help before that, but if he doesn't then we'll build a fire with driftwood. I can see matches in Meg's Marvellous Bag. We'll sing songs and tell each other stories and then we'll lie on these…yep, thermal blankets…and we'll wait until they come. Is that okay with you, Henry?'

'I…guess…'

It was okay with Meg, too. It sounded like a workable plan—the only hiccup being…

Charlie.

We'll wait for Meg's boss to realise she's no longer in radio contact…

Charlie's charter boats were supposed to check in every hour, acknowledging to Charlie that boats and punters were safe. Meg couldn't remember the last time she'd seen Charlie monitor those calls. The calls were made—most of his skippers were punctilious—but they were made to an empty control room.

Charlie was always on the pier, chatting to the locals. He watched his boats come in every night. If Meg was due in tonight and didn't show, Charlie would notice. The trouble was, Meg wasn't due back tonight. Or tomorrow.

She closed her eyes.

'Bad?' Matt asked sympathetically.

And she thought, *He's not going to be sympathetic when I tell him I work for one of the world's shonkiest charter companies.*

But it was no use telling him now, especially not when he'd just reassured Henry.

'I'm okay,' she muttered and lowered her head again. It must be the smoke still making her feel sick. 'We'll all be okay. Eventually.'

CHAPTER THREE

FIFTEEN MINUTES LATER they reached their destination.

The combination of medication and salt air had worked their magic. Meg's lungs felt almost clear.

She still wasn't in control, though. Matt had taken over. The letterhead on the documents she'd read had been embossed with the words *McLellan Corporation*. Matt's name? Her first impression had been wealth and command, and she was now adding skill to the mix. Wherever he'd learned it, he'd acquired knowledge of the sea and small boats. He was now in charge, and the feeling was almost overwhelming.

How long had it been since anyone had taken charge of her world? Not since her grandpa had got sick. Even as a child Meg had learned to be leaned on. Her grandparents had been gutted when her parents had been killed. If she cried, they couldn't handle it. She'd had to act cheerful even when things were dire.

When she was sixteen her gran had died, too, and Grandpa had pretty much fallen to pieces. That was when she'd decided to quit school and go fishing with him. She'd cajoled him back to enjoying life.

It was only when he was gone that she realised how restricted her own life had become. She could heave craypots. She could count punters in and out of charter boats and she could cope with boats in heavy seas.

Was that what she wanted for the rest of her life?

At twenty-eight, what other choices did she have?

Oh, for heaven's sake, why was she thinking that now? They'd reached the outcrop. Matt was steering carefully—because the boat was inflatable and the rubber could rip on any one of these sharp rocks—into the tiny cove. There was a stony beach.

She needed to stop thinking of the complications of her life. More immediately, she needed to stop thinking how good it was to let this guy take over—and how good he looked while he did it—and start being useful.

She hauled up the legs of her jeans, checked the bottom and jumped out into knee-deep water. Beaching the tender wasn't an option on these sharp stones.

The cove was sheltered from the prevailing winds, and she could see to the bottom.

'I didn't mean you to do that,' Matt said, sounding displeased. 'I thought we'd run her up on the beach.'

'And rupture the membrane?'

'Instead of your feet? Yes. And we won't have any more use for her. We're hardly here to re-provision and set off for the mainland.'

'But why wreck a perfectly good inflatable?' She wasn't about to tell him it might well be needed again. *Focus on now.*

She clicked her fingers. Boof jumped into her arms and she carted him to shore. Ouch, these stones were sharp! Her shoes were...with the remains of *Bertha.*

Henry next. 'Will you let me carry you to Boof?' she asked him.

'I'll take him,' Matt said but she shook her head.

'Can you stay at the tiller until we're unloaded? If we get an unexpected swell the boat might be damaged.'

His eyes had narrowed. 'So that matters?'

'That matters.'

He got it. But he glanced at Henry and didn't comment.

'You're not fit enough to...'

'Lift Henry? Of course I am. Henry, I bet you don't weigh as much as Boof. Will you let me carry you? You could jump in and walk, like me, but the water's a bit cold. I think I saw a seal somewhere round the back of these rocks. Boof might show you if you ask.'

But the strangeness of their situation was taking its toll. Henry clutched his seat and held. 'Our boat burned,' he said flatly.

'It did,' Matt told him. 'It was a bad accident and we're lucky Meg brought this little boat along. Now we need to stay here for a bit.'

'Will you stay?' Henry demanded and Meg heard raw fear. Matt, then, was more than just his mother's employer to this little boy. He was the only link Henry had to his past, to an unknown future.

And Matt obviously got that, too. 'I'll stay with you,' he said solemnly, and Meg thought what choice did he have? But Matt didn't waste time explaining. He simply promised. 'I said I'll stay with you until you're with your grandma and I will. No question, Henry. Now, will you let Miss O'Hara…?'

'Meg,' said Meg.

'Will you let Meg carry you to the shore?'

There was a moment's thought. Then: 'Yes,' Henry said. 'Yes, please, Miss O'Hara.'

'Meg,' Meg said again.

'Yes, please, Meg,' Henry said and looped his arms around Meg's neck and allowed her to carry him.

And why that made her feel like bursting into tears, she had no idea.

She was amazing.

Half an hour ago she'd been coughing so hard she'd been retching. Now it was as if this were nothing out of the ordinary.

He couldn't fault her.

While he kept the boat steady she gathered the bag and carted that to shore, as well. Finally she agreed to allow him out of the boat.

'We need to take the motor off and cart that up the beach, then the water and the bench seats, and then carry the tender itself,' she told him. 'I don't know about you, but I'm not strong enough to cart it with the motor attached.'

'We can't just anchor?'

'Too risky—these rocks are sharp. Leave your socks on by the way.' She was already disconnecting the motor.

'So we're being careful of the tender...why?' Henry was out of earshot now. Boof had met him on the shore and they were both tentatively looking for seals. With his hand on the dog's collar, Henry seemed to have found courage.

'If we can get it onto the sand it'll make a comfy place to sleep,' Meg told him. 'With the thermal blankets, we'll be snug as bugs in rugs.'

'We're not expecting rescue tonight?'

'No.'

'I would have thought,' he said almost conversationally, 'that a burned boat in the middle of Bass Strait, with three stranded passengers and one dog, might mean immediate search and rescue.' He kicked off his shoes, hitched his trousers and was over the side. 'You hold the boat. I'll cart the motor in.'

She was more than happy to let him. Someone had to hold the boat. She'd heaved an outboard motor before, but she was five feet four and slightly built, and even a lifetime of heaving craypots wouldn't have prevented her from staggering.

So she could only be grateful as Matt disconnected bolts, heaved the motor into his arms and strode through the shallows to the beach.

What sort of New York financier and lawyer was this? One who worked out, obviously.

She'd given them both sou'westers and life-jackets as they'd boarded the boat. Henry was still wearing his, but Matt's was on the floor of the tender with his shoes. She thought fleetingly of his gorgeous leather jacket, replaced with the sou'wester. It'd be ashes by now, but he wasn't worrying about a jacket.

He'd hiked up his trousers and rolled his shirt-sleeves. He'd taken her advice and was still wearing socks. Another guy might look naff in bare legs and socks, but not this man. He was all hard muscle, lean, toned, ripped. He carted the motor as if it were nothing and, as she held the boat steady, Meg had a sudden fantasy of what it'd be like to be carried by such a man. To be held in those arms…against that chest…

Um…not.

'Earth to Meg,' Matt said as he returned, hauling her back to reality. 'You were explaining why rescue isn't imminent.'

Time for confession. Just say it.

'The radio's not in the bag, nor is our emergency transmitter,' she admitted. 'Someone's head will roll for that.' Probably not, though, she thought. Charlie was her boss and she was hardly in a position to complain. 'Our phones don't work out here. We have no way of saying we're stranded.'

'I'd imagine your boss will be checking your position, though. If you don't make it to Garnett tonight, surely he'll notice.'

And there was no way she could sugar-coat this. 'Don't bet on it. Monitoring the radio takes staff or work, both of which Charlie keeps to a minimum. The reason you were able to hire *Bertha* at such short notice is that we're not a flash operation. In fact—' *go on, say it* '—Charlie runs on the smell of an oily rag. If there's a corner to cut, he'll cut it. *Bertha*'s due back to port by Monday. On Monday night he'll start wondering.'

'But not before.'

'Probably not.'

He didn't comment. Instead he heaved the water container from under the seat and carried that to the beach as well, then did the same with the removable seats.

A lawyer with muscles.

She thought, suddenly, idiotically, of fairy tales she'd read as a kid, and romance novels since. It had seemed to her that a hero would be rich and handsome. She'd thought mistily that a hero might even heave her craypots for her.

And here he was, rich—presumably, if his name headed a prestigious Manhattan law firm. Handsome... Yeah, tick that. Now he was carting the motor and water as if they were featherweights.

Fantasy plus. She almost grinned but then he was striding back, gripping the boat's bow, readying to lift it and carry it to shore.

He couldn't do this alone. It wasn't the weight; it was the sheer size of the thing.

'So we're dependent on Peggy,' he said, almost conversationally.

She'd already thought of that, with some relief. Peggy Lakey. Henry's grandmother.

'I assume you told her your travel plans,' she said.

'I did. She knows we landed in Melbourne this morning. She knows we were using this charter company and she's expecting us by dark.'

'And she has a radio.' They were heaving the boat upward, out of danger of scraping, working as a team. Once again she had the impression that this guy was used to boats, used to the sea. Used to work?

'It was a shaky connection this morning,' Matt said. He was moving backward. She had the easy option of walking forward. 'But I'd imagine if we're not there by dark then she'll call Charlie.'

'And if Charlie doesn't answer?'

'Is that possible?'

'The local football team's reached the finals,' she said dryly. 'Yes, it is.'

'And you work for this man?'

She couldn't defend herself. She didn't even try. They had the boat out of the water now, carrying it over the rocks to the strip of sand beneath the cliff. They set it down with care and Meg breathed a sigh of relief. The boat was safe. They had water and supplies. This wasn't a total disaster.

'So Peggy?' she ventured. She knew a little about Peggy Lakey, an elderly woman who'd bought Garnett Island years ago. She was said to be reclusive—she'd have to be to live on Garnett—but the fishermen who carted her supplies over had always been impressed with her.

'She seems no-nonsense,' Matt told her. 'Charlie assured me—and I assured Peggy—that we'd be there before dark. I'm thinking she'll contact the rescue services soon after. This is her grand-son, after all.'

'Does she want him?' Her gaze moved to Henry. The little boy had found a shallow rock pool. He was pointing to something in its depths and Boof, bless his doggy heart, was paying attention.

It'd be minnows. The thought almost made her smile. Years of devoted hunting, and Boof had never caught one.

She watched kid and dog watching the fish darting below the surface. Matt was watching, too.

'Does his grandmother want him?' she asked again.

'I think so.'

'You think so?' That jolted her. What the...? 'You bring him all the way here—and you *think so*?'

'There's no choice,' he said, heavily now. He wasn't taking his eyes off the child. 'Amanda's will left him in the care of his grandmother. Peg-gy's expressed willingness to take him.'

'But she wouldn't fetch him.'

'No.'

'Does he even know her?'

'They write,' he said. 'He tells me he gets a

letter every week, old-style, in an envelope with a stamp. She sends Polaroid pictures of the island. That's what's in his backpack—letters and pictures she's been sending for years. I've seen them. She also makes radio telephone calls when she can. He feels like he knows her and there's no doubt she cares.'

That was something at least, but she hadn't finished probing.

'Has he ever met her?'

'Will you cut it out?' His voice was suddenly laced with anger. 'The paperwork's in order. It's your job to get us there safely, and might I remind you that you're doing an appalling job of it.'

'And so are you,' she snapped back. 'Your job's to get him to his grandma, so we've both failed. Get over it.'

'I'm over it. Just don't make me responsible...'

'For what?'

'For bringing him here.' He closed his eyes and ran his fingers through his hair, a gesture of total fatigue. 'Look, this is a no-win situation,' he said. 'Amanda was an excellent lawyer but an appalling mother. According to office gossip, when she turned forty she decided she wanted a child like some people decide they want a puppy. She's been paying as little as she could get away with for child care. During term breaks Henry would be alone in her office for hours. Now she's dead and she has no friends close enough to care. Henry has a grandma he's never met and no one else.'

'So how come he's never met her?'

'Because Peggy hasn't seen Amanda for years, either,' he said wearily. 'Peggy told me the outline when I contacted her. She's Australian. She was married to an American. He died a couple of years back, but the marriage broke up when Amanda was in her teens. Peggy came home to Australia. She says she tried to keep in contact, but Amanda wasn't interested. When Henry was born Peggy doubled her efforts. Maybe she knew what sort of mother Amanda would make. I gather Amanda allowed Peggy to write to him and speak to him occasionally via her not very satisfactory radio connection, but that's all. Now she's all he has.'

'He has you, though,' Meg said, thinking what she was hearing wasn't weariness. This was desolation for a child left with nothing.

Desolation from a high-flying businessman who'd dropped everything to bring a kid to his grandma.

Her first impression of this guy had been arrogance. He'd reacted with astonishment when she'd questioned his right to bring Henry to the island, and what he was paying Charlie was astounding. He was obviously accustomed to throwing money and watching minions jump.

But now… Yes, the need to control was still there, but despite it she was starting to like what she saw around the edges. Even before the fire she'd been sensing helplessness in the way he was caring for Henry. Now he was stranded, shaken from his controlled world, his desolation was exposed, and it touched something deep within.

'It's okay.' Her hand went to his shoulder, a touch of reassurance. 'I bet Peggy's lovely. Writing real letters every week… That's awesome. We'll land on the island, she'll love him to bits and they'll live happily ever after.'

'Yeah,' he said. She'd tugged her hand back but the look he gave her… It was as if he couldn't figure her out. 'But meanwhile…'

'Meanwhile we collect driftwood before it starts getting dark,' she said. 'A fire will cheer us up. It's a warm night. With the seats removed from the boat we have a comfy bed, and we have thermal blankets. We have the means to make a fire and we have food.'

'Muesli bars?' he said dubiously, stooping to check her bag.

'Yes, but some of them have chocolate coating. Yay.' She investigated with him. 'Plus, here's a fishing line and a lure. By the time you have the fire going, I'll have fish to cook.'

'Right,' he said dryly.

'You doubt me? I may not be able to deliver you to your island without sending you up in flames but I was born with a fishing line in my hands. Watch this space.'

'And we'd cook it how?'

'Seaweed and ash,' she said. 'Don't they teach you anything in law school?'

'Apparently not,' he said faintly. 'Henry,' he called. 'Do you want to help me make a fire, or watch Meg fish?'

And that was a no-brainer. Henry headed straight for Meg. And as dog and boy clambered over the rocks toward them, Matt thought, *He looks almost happy.*

He'd never seen Henry look happy.

It was almost enough to make a burned boat and a night on a deserted island worthwhile.

CHAPTER FOUR

THE ROCKS AROUND the cove looked as if they'd been a driftwood catchment for years. Matt lit a fire and then went down to the rocks to watch what was happening. Henry was riveted, and as soon as he arrived, so was Matt.

As Matt settled on a rock beside them, Meg seamlessly included him in a fishing lesson.

They'd been catching fish too small to keep, she explained. She was teaching Henry how to throw them back.

'Barbs damage their mouths,' she told him. 'They often don't survive. An unbarbed hook rarely does lasting damage but it needs skill. The trick is to feel the moment the hook's taken. If you keep the pressure steady on the way in, the fish won't get off. Henry, there's one on the line now. Here it comes. You know what to do.'

There'd been a netting insert on the inside of the emergency bag. He'd seen Meg tie it to drift-wood sticks to make a net. Henry had ditched his shoes and socks. Now he waded into the water and scooped the fish like an expert.

'It's nearly big enough,' he announced. He stared into the net at the flopping fish and then he glanced at Matt's foot. 'Meg says it's got to be as big as your foot before we eat it. I don't think this is.'

'Not quite,' Meg said, inspecting their catch. 'It's a good one, though. Do you want to try to get the hook out yourself this time? Remember what I showed you.'

'Yes,' Henry said, and while Meg held the fish he cautiously removed the hook. A surgeon couldn't have taken more care.

'Can I let it go?' he asked.

'Of course.' She manoeuvred the slippery fish into Henry's hold and Henry waded back out into the water.

'Goodbye, fish,' he said solemnly. 'Meg says your mouth won't hurt for long. Don't go near them hooks any more.'

He slid the fish into the water and Meg tossed the line back out. Pretty far for a girl, Matt thought, and grinned to himself at his blatantly sexist thought. Pretty far for a fisherman? Fisherwoman? Whatever, that was what she obviously was.

They settled down again. Meg and Henry were side by side on the rock. Boof had been sniffing seaweed. He came back to them now and Henry's spare arm wrapped around the dog's neck.

And Matt thought, What a gift.

For the last two weeks Henry had been limp with shock and with fear. He'd hardly spoken during the journey here. He'd been totally self-effacing and then he'd had to cope with the fire. Matt had done what he could to reassure him but it had been Meg who'd hauled him out of his frozen acceptance of things a child shouldn't have to face.

The sun was sinking but there was still enough warmth in it to give comfort. Henry was dangling his feet in the water. He was watching his line, intent, fascinated.

What looked like a tiny stingray drifted near his toes. Henry lifted his feet in alarm but Meg reacted by showing him the beauty of the little creature. She explained how it steered with its 'wings'. How the fins on its tail, the only part breaking the surface, made it look a bit like a Loch Ness monster in miniature.

'Or a diplocaulus,' Henry ventured and Matt thought… What?

But the conversation continued without a

pause. 'It could be a very small diplocaulus,' Meg said, appearing to consider. 'Some pictures I've seen have fin-like feathering on their tails like this.'

'What's a diplocaulus?' he asked, and both Meg and Henry looked at him as if they were astounded someone wouldn't know.

'It was a kind of shark,' Henry said with patience. 'It lived about three hundred million years ago, and it had a head like a boomerang. That made it hard for other things to swallow it.'

'Which seems a good reason to have a boomerang-shaped head,' Meg said, and she grinned.

And he thought, *She's beautiful. No, more than beautiful. She's stunning.*

She wasn't his kind of woman. Not in a million years.

The women Matt associated with were part of his corporate world, socially elite. There'd never been anyone special enough to make him think of long-term commitment, but at some time in the future he imagined one of these women could become his wife. She'd be a woman who fitted seamlessly into the world he moved in, with her own career, her own identity, but who understood the needs his high-pressured job put on him.

Meg was so much out of that mould that maybe it was like the... What had they been talking of? The diplocaulus. With her bare feet, her torn jeans and stained windcheater, with her freckled nose, her badly cut copper curls, her wide green eyes... It was as if she'd come from a different planet from the one he inhabited.

But she was, indeed, beautiful.

'What?' she said and he realised he was staring.

'I... Sorry. It's just...the women in the circles I move in don't fish.'

'Is that a rule?'

He gathered his wits—with difficulty. 'We don't have a lot of places to fish in Manhattan.'

'And yet you know your way round boats.'

'My family's always had a home in the Hamptons.'

'Where's that?

'It's on the South Fork of Long Island.' He reached for his phone to show her a map. And remembered. There wasn't a lot of internet access here.

She saw the motion and her smile returned. It really was dazzling. Her nose was snub. She had the remains of zinc on her nose—she'd insisted they use expensive sun lotion on the boat but she obviously preferred the old-fashioned kind. It must have its limitations, though. Her eyes crinkled at the edges, presumably because of too much exposure to water-reflected sun. A fault?

No. She was definitely beautiful.

'So the Hamptons are where your mum and dad live?'

'We use it for holidays.'

'Gorgeous. Did you have it when you were a kid?'

'We've had it for generations.'

'There are holiday cottages like that in Rowan Bay,' she said. 'They look like they're held up with string, but generation after generation arrive, summer after summer. A stovetop, bunks, a cold shower and the beach at the door. They love them. Is that what your place is like?'

'Um…no.' McLellan Place?

'It does run to hot water,' he admitted.

'Luxury.' The smile seemed irrepressible. 'We have hot water at our…at my place, too.'

He got the *our* versus *my*. He saw the cloud.

'Is that the place you shared with your grandfather?'

Where had that come from? Asking personal questions of someone he'd hired as a marine taxi driver wasn't his style. She wasn't a taxi driver now, though. She had her arm around Henry while he was concentrating on his line. What did you pay for making a kid relax? Personal interest seemed the least he could do, and, besides, he genuinely wanted to know.

And she told him. 'I did live with my grandpa,' she said. 'I told you back at the office. He died six months ago and I miss him. I guess you feel exactly the same, Henry, missing your mom and all.'

And that pretty much took his breath away.

Henry hadn't talked about his mother. Not once. Henry had been drawing dinosaurs before they'd left the office the day his mother had died, big dinosaurs on a huge sketchpad his mother had left him. He'd kept drawing in the days that had followed, but the dinosaurs had become very small.

So now Matt expected Henry to close down, as he'd closed every time his mother had been mentioned. But he was still encircled by Meg's arm. Boof was nestled on his other side. They were watching the float above the hook on the end of the fishing line. No pressure.

'I miss her at night,' Henry whispered. 'She always comes in to say goodnight, even if it's really late. I make myself stay awake. Me and

Teddy. Now we stay awake and stay awake and she doesn't come.'

There was a gut clencher.

His heart seemed to close down in sympathy. Empathy?

Suddenly he was remembering years of waiting for his socialite parents to come home. Their steps on the stairs.

Goodnight, darling...

The flashback hit hard. He winced. This was not about him. He hadn't lost his parents when he was a child. His father had died three years ago, of a coronary probably brought on by years of too much wine, too many cigars. His mother was still in his orbit although rarely coming close, expending her energy in keeping her place in New York's social hierarchy.

He struggled to think of something to say. Anything.

But Meg was before him. 'I bet your mom still says goodnight to you,' she said, almost conversationally.

'She's dead.'

'So's my grandpa. At night, in bed, knowing he's not in the next room, it hurts so much sometimes I feel like my chest is about to burst. But if I close my eyes, if I sing to myself, a song

Grandpa taught me, or if I think of something we both liked—like dinosaurs—then I know that somehow Grandpa's still with me. Not really, of course, not in the way he was there when he told me off for wearing muddy shoes in the house. Just…it feels like he still loves me. I feel him when I need him. Henry, I reckon you could feel your mom like that.'

'My chest hurts, too,' Henry whispered.

Matt thought, Ditto.

'Your grandma will tell you stories about your mom,' he managed. 'Your grandma loves your mom, Henry.'

'And I wouldn't be the least bit surprised if your grandma says goodnight to you every night, as well,' Meg added. 'But meanwhile, Henry, that float's wobbling. I reckon there's a fish about to bite.'

'Yes!' said Henry, lighting up again. Fish were immediate. Fish were now. He stared intently at the definitely wobbling float. Conversation over.

Matt expected Meg to turn her attention to the float as well. Instead she turned her gaze to him and her look was…thoughtful? Speculative?

More. The way he was feeling about Henry… In Meg's eyes he could almost read the same, but for some reason it didn't seem like sympathy toward Henry. Her emotions seemed directed to him.

How much was she seeing?

This was crazy. It was ridiculous to think this woman could sense the emptiness he shared with Henry.

And he didn't share it. Not any more. It was simply that Henry's loneliness had struck a chord.

But had that loneliness killed something? He'd tried his best over the last couple of weeks to find some way to comfort Henry, to give him time out from his grief, but his approaches had been stilted. He knew they had. Henry had become more and more exhausted with his fear of an unknown future, and Matt had found no way to break through.

This woman, though… From the time she'd grasped Henry's hand and shaken it, adult to adult, to now… She'd been giving Henry time out, and she'd been doing it almost instinctively. How did she do that?

And what was with the way she looked at him? As if he needed sympathy, too?

'I'll check the fire,' he said, a bit too roughly, and her smile came back. But this time her smile was different.

'You do that,' she said. 'We'll need it to stay warm tonight.' And then she turned back to Henry as the float plunged underneath the water. 'Henry, we've got one. Ooh, look at him. Trevally! Careful, hold steady but no tugging. Hooray, Henry, we might be about to meet our dinner.'

CHAPTER FIVE

GIVEN THE CIRCUMSTANCES, it was an excellent dinner.

Meg was obviously an old hand at cooking fish. She wrapped it whole in damp seaweed, then buried it in hot ash. Half an hour later she dug it out and lifted the charred seaweed away. They used their fingers to lift away chunks of the succulent flesh and Matt thought he'd never tasted such fish.

Even Henry, who'd eaten birdlike portions over the last couple of weeks, enjoyed his. It might have been because he was sharing with Boof. The fish they'd caught was big enough for them all, but Meg discussed rules with Henry before they ate.

'Boof eats doggy kibbles. You fed him on the boat so he shouldn't be hungry. Sometimes, though, I give him me-food as a treat, but he's not allowed to ask. I eat three bites and give him one. Then three more bites and one for him.'

It sounded an unlikely rule. Matt raised an eyebrow and Meg smiled. As Henry started on his first bite, Meg sent him a conspiratorial wink.

She had him entranced. He watched Henry do the three-one rule and he thought, How clever was that? She'd seamlessly persuaded Henry to eat three pieces of fish before he could feed Boof. The fish went down, then Henry shared his muesli bar.

With Henry fed, safe, warm, the little boy leaned against Meg and listened as she told him about the evening star, just starting to appear as the light faded.

She told him of an Aboriginal legend: two beautiful sisters, escaping danger, one flying all the way into the night sky to become the evening star, then using her powers to watch over her earthbound sister and keep her safe.

Meg was sure she was also watching over them.

Yep, he was definitely entranced.

The dark descended and Henry fell asleep. Meg went to lift him, to carry him to the tender but Matt was before her.

'Give me a break,' he told her. 'I've watched you save us from fire, provide us with a campsite, catch our dinner. I need at least one opportunity to be manly.'

'Or one excuse to give Henry a hug,' Meg said as he lifted Henry into his arms and that made him blink, too.

She made him transparent.

She made him feel…vulnerable?

That was dumb, but as he carried the sleeping child to the tender, as he settled him on its air-filled base and tucked a thermal blanket around him, making sure Teddy was close, his feeling of vulnerability increased.

Why?

It was obvious, he told himself. He was somewhere in the Southern Ocean, stranded after a fire that could easily have killed them.

Matt McLellan was a man to whom control was everything. He'd been born to inherited wealth, and his financial acumen had seen that wealth increase tenfold. He was one of Manhattan's movers and shakers.

But this situation wasn't frightening. Yes, they were stranded but Peggy would contact the authorities. They had fresh water, they had fire and they had food. Thanks to Meg and her blessed bag.

And that was where his thoughts paused. Meg.

Meg, who worked for a company that had nearly killed him.

Meg, who made a little boy chuckle.

Meg, who looked at him as if she saw inside.

That was being dumb. She didn't see anything, or, if she did, maybe it was just that shock had meant his face was less than impassive.

But the thought still had him unnerved. He spent longer than he needed making sure Henry's blanket was tucked around him, giving himself space. He needed to focus on imperatives. Making contact with the outside world.

But for some reason his thoughts were stalling there as well. For the time being they were safe. The weather was kind. Something about this situation—or was it something about Meg?— was helping Henry put aside the trauma of the last weeks. To be honest, Matt was feeling the same. He wouldn't mind a little longer...

Or not. Was he thinking? He needed to hand Henry to his grandmother, make sure he was safe and then get back to the world he knew. He didn't need to get any more involved. The last two weeks had hauled him out of his comfort zone, facing emotion he didn't know how to deal with.

Meg knew how to deal with it. She was warm,

funny, empathic. She was all the things he wasn't. She provided things he'd been trained since birth not to need.

He turned back to the fire. Meg was sitting on a driftwood log. Her face was lit by the flames. She looked...

It didn't matter how she looked. It didn't matter that something within him was telling him to ignore what he needed to do and go sit beside Meg.

Moving on. He rose and headed for her blessed bag, stooping to forage.

'What are you looking for?' she asked. 'Don't you dare eat the orange-and-chocolate muesli bars. I've saved them for breakfast. If you eat them now, we'll be reduced to the bran-and-oatmeal ones.'

'I'm looking for something to save us from bran and oatmeal. Yes!' He tugged flares from the base of the bag.

'I already thought about the flares,' she said diffidently. 'But it seems unsafe.'

'Because Peggy might see them from Garnett?' He guessed her thinking on this one. Peggy seeing was one thing. What Peggy did with that knowledge was another.

'Our rescue's not urgent,' Meg explained.

'We're within sight of Garnett Island. It's still maybe half an hour away in a decent boat, but a flare could well be seen over there. But Peggy'll have been expecting her grandson and by now she'll be terrified something's happened. I'm hoping she'll have contacted the authorities, which means they'll be organising a search, but that won't start until dawn. If she sees a flare now, it could be from a sinking boat. If she thinks that… If it was my grandson, I'd be in a boat, heading out, no matter how elderly I am or what condition my boat is in.'

'I agree,' he said, setting the flares in a row. 'Twelve flares. Excellent.'

'So what I just said?'

'Factored in, but my plan is to try to stop her spending the night out of her mind with worry. I've been trying to put myself in her shoes. If I were Peggy, I'd have radioed the authorities but I wouldn't stop there. I'd be scanning the sea, waiting, hoping. So my current plan is to use more of this excellent driftwood to light three burning fires along the top of the cliff. Spaced so they look as if they've been deliberately lit and they can't be mistaken for a burning boat. I imagine they'll still be hard to see from Garnett, but if we light the flares, I hope she'll see a flash and focus. The fires should be spots of light visible by the naked eye and easily seen with field glasses. She sounded sensible when I talked to her. I imagine she'll figure where we are, which means tomorrow we'll be rescued without the need for an expensive search. And she'll sleep…not easy but maybe she won't be in total meltdown.'

There was a moment's silence. A long one. And then, for some reason, Meg's eyes welled. She swiped a tear away with what seemed anger, and when she spoke again her voice was choked. 'That's…that's a great plan. And kind.'

'Self-preserving. We'll be rescued sooner.'

'You know we'll be rescued. But to think of Peggy… Matt, that's brilliant. I'll help you collect driftwood. We just need to climb…'

'No,' he said forcibly. 'Meg, there's not a snowball's chance in hell that you're doing more tonight. I can still hear the smoke in your lungs. There's no way you're climbing cliffs.'

'I'm responsible,' she said miserably. 'You paid me, and I got you into this mess.'

'I paid your boss, and your boss was paying you to be at the wheel of an unseaworthy boat. We're in the same mess, except you've been injured and I haven't. Also… Meg, Henry's asleep and if he wakes, do you think I want him alone? He needs one of us here and you're elected.'

And then, because he could see a tear tracking its way down her smoke-stained face in the firelight—he didn't know what that tear was about but he was stopping it regardless—he cupped her chin and wiped it away with his finger.

'Put the albuterol in your pocket in case you need it,' he told her. 'Then get into the tender with Henry and stay there. Tug another thermal blanket around you. Hug Boof. Hug Henry if he needs it. But see if you can sleep. I'll keep the fires going, Meg, and I'll keep watch.'

'In case of werewolves?' She was struggling to sound light.

'Yep. No werewolf will get past me and my trusty...' He searched the ground for something weapon-like and found a flare. 'Me and my trusty flare. And I have twelve of 'em.'

And she chuckled. It was a choked kind of chuckle but it sounded...okay.

'Take Boof,' she managed. 'He's good at werewolves.'

'Really?'

'In all the years I've had him, I haven't been troubled by a werewolf once.'

'That's a huge recommendation,' he said. For

some reason he was still cupping her chin. Smiling down at her. 'But you know what? I'll cope with my own werewolves. Boof's staying here to cope with yours.'

She followed orders and it felt wrong.

Or maybe not wrong. Strange. Someone else was in charge of her world.

She should feel terrible. She'd lost the boat. She'd almost killed her paying customers and she knew already that Charlie would put the blame squarely on her. If this guy was to sue— and he was a hotshot US lawyer so that was well within the realms of possibility—she already knew she'd be thrown to the wolves.

To Matt's werewolves. Unaccountably, she found she was smiling.

He'd given her a job: snuggle down in the tender and take care of Henry.

She did just that. She hauled a thermal blanket around her. Henry muttered a little in his sleep. She settled beside him, moved closer and put her arms around him.

Boof jumped in on her feet. Um, maybe not. 'Out,' she murmured and he obligingly jumped out. She clicked her fingers to the side of the boat and he settled as close as he could. She could reach out and touch him if she wanted.

Matt had stoked up their camp fire before he left. Its flames were still easing the dark.

'We're warm and we're safe and Matt's looking after us,' she murmured to Henry and she felt him nestle closer still.

Matt's looking after us.

It was a good thought. Maybe it was even a great thought.

She closed her eyes and felt herself drift into sleep.

Peggy noticed.

Bless her.

Thirty minutes after he lit his fires, after his first flare lit the night, just before he was about to use his second, he saw an answering glow from Garnett Island. She must have heaved combustibles together fast. He had no field glasses and Garnett was some way off but he saw the faint, answering glow and he relaxed.

It was the most primitive communication he could think of but it was enough. Peggy had seen his fires. She'd know where they were and her answering fire meant she'd send help. He wished he could let her know they were all safe, but he hoped she'd assume it.

He wouldn't light more flares—they could be seen as a plea for immediate help. He'd done all he could. He could head back to the tender and see if he could get some sleep.

He made his way carefully down the cliff, thinking how glad he was he hadn't needed Meg's help. The rocks were small, shifting, unstable. He wanted her where she was, snug in the tender. Their camp fire was a glow below him and as he climbed down he was aware of a surge of something strange.

As if…he was heading home?

It was a weird feeling, and it didn't ease when he reached the bottom. Boof lifted his head and gave him a token tail wag as he neared the little boat. He kept his flashlight on, but low and turned aside so he wouldn't wake the occupants.

Meg was cradling Henry, even in sleep. She had him tucked into the crook of her arm. Taking comfort or giving it? He couldn't be sure.

They were huddled against the tender's side and there was space left beside her. Boof could have fitted, he thought, but with a flash of insight he realised what Meg had done.

She'd left space for him.

A hero wouldn't climb into the tender with them, he thought wryly. A hero had no need for that sense of comfort. Surely he should stay awake, tending the camp fire, keeping watch over his charges, keeping werewolves at bay.

But there was nary a werewolf, and suddenly Meg stirred. She was on her back, one arm around Henry, and now her spare arm reached up toward him.

'Hey,' she murmured, half-asleep. 'Time to rest?'

'Peggy saw our fires. She lit one herself to show us she's seen.'

'Excellent.' Her voice was still slurred. 'So come on in, Matt McLellan.'

There was hardly room. Widthways, yes, but lengthways his feet would either have to rest up on the sides or they'd have to squash.

She smiled up at him. That hand still reached up.

He smiled back down and decided to squash.

She woke and she couldn't breathe.

Her first thought was that she was choking. Her second was that she couldn't wake Henry. She choked into her sleeve, fighting for breath. Her whole body was trembling.

She mustn't wake…

But Matt's arm was suddenly around her, tugging her to sit upward. Henry was waking beside her, jerked into alarm.

She sat and buckled and coughed and fought for breath, and then Matt was lifting her up, out of the boat, cradling her in his arms.

'Henry, it's okay,' he said. 'Meg got smoke in her chest today but she'll be okay. She just needs to cough it out.'

She wasn't okay. She felt as if she were dying. Somehow, almost by instinct, she forced herself to snap her fingers to Boof, make a gesture…

Boof was a great dog. He looked up at his mistress, his head on one side while he figured what she was trying to tell him—and then he stepped carefully into the tender. He plonked down beside Henry. Henry's arm came around him and the little boy settled again into sleep.

Which meant Meg could concentrate on breathing. Which wasn't happening. She was fighting, her breath coming in sharp, short rasps. Her chest hurt. Her whole body was shaking.

Matt was carrying her over to the embers of their fire, swearing.

'It's okay, sweetheart. The albuterol's in your pocket? Right, let's get you breathing.'

He settled on a rock and held the albuterol to her lips.

She sucked like she was drowning. It wasn't helping. It wasn't…

And then Matt was grabbing one of the bags of muesli bars. The bars were unceremoniously tipped and the bag held to her lips.

'Meg, I'm thinking this is a panic attack. Let's treat it as that. Breathe into the bag.'

Panic attack? She'd never had such a thing. This was a heart attack or worse. But Matt was holding the bag to her lips. 'Breathe,' he said. 'Fill the bag and then take it in again. Slow as you can. Do it, Meg.'

And his authority cut through her terror. He was still holding her, cradling her like a child, but his voice brooked no argument.

She breathed.

The bag forced her to slow. She had to make it inflate. She was trying so hard…

'Great job, Meg. Keep going. One after the other.'

He held her while she breathed. She just… breathed.

And slowly, miraculously, the panic eased. The pain in her chest backed off.

She was still shaking. If Matt let her go she

would have sobbed with distress but he did no such thing. He held her close until finally the shakes subsided. Until finally she was brave enough to put the bag down, to try to talk. She was mortified.

'I can't... I don't...'

'It's okay,' he said, gently but firmly. 'You're okay. Meg, I don't think it was the smoke. I've seen a full-blown panic attack before. It was a colleague when she'd realised she'd forgotten to register a share transfer. Half a million lost in an instant. You, waking up to the memory of a burning boat, with lives at stake... That's so much worse. You have every right to panic.'

'I don't... It felt...'

'Like you were suffocating? We called the paramedics for Donna. They said with the bag you're forced to focus on breathing. You can see what's happening with the rise and fall of the bag, and you don't have room for the rest of the stuff. Neat, huh? I love it when a plan works.'

She didn't reply. She couldn't yet, but his steady voice, his calm, had her world settling. The tremors hadn't completely eased but the panic had.

Had she had a nightmare? She vaguely re-membered waking to the memory of flames, of choking smoke, of looking out of the hatch and knowing the lives entrusted to her were in peril.

It was over. Past. Why should she be shaking now?

'I think it's adrenalin,' Matt said, as if he could hear what she was thinking. 'In an emergency adrenalin kicks in. You responded brilliantly. You got us here safe. You comforted Henry, you made him feel like all was well with his world and then you flaked out with exhaustion. And the adrenalin dropped and the fear found its way to the surface.'

'It was my fault. I should have—'

'What, inspected every part of the boat for faults? Nothing's perfect, Meg. Even luxury limos break down.'

'They don't burst into flames.'

'I bet they do. I bet somewhere in the echelons of motoring history someone's standing beside a half-million-dollar car while the engine puffs smoke.' And then as she relaxed, just a little bit, he hugged her tighter. 'You did great, Meg, and it's all great from here on. Peggy will have contacted the authorities. I wouldn't be surprised if we have helicopters hovering over us at dawn, so how about we sleep now?'

And before she realised what he was about,

he lifted her and carried her bodily back to the tender.

Henry, reassured by Boof's solid presence, had drifted off to sleep again. The big dog was still lying beside him, taking up the entire floor space. Now he opened one eye and gazed up at them suspiciously. As well as he might. 'Boof, out,' Matt said and Boof did exactly that.

'He only does...what I say,' she managed.

'He only does what's good for his mistress.' Matt lowered her onto the rubber and tucked a space blanket around her. 'Now, sleep.'

'Matt?'

'Mmm?'

'There's room for you.'

'I'll sleep by the fire.'

'No.' The panic was still in the recesses of her mind. It was because the tender was more comfortable, she told herself. He'd sleep better on the inflatable surface.

But she knew it was more than that. He'd held her and the terror had receded. If he could just... hold her...

And he got it. He stooped and touched her on the cheek. It was the gentlest of touches and why it should send a frisson of pure heat through her...

There was no reason, but as he smiled and slid into the tender beside her, as he tucked her under his arm, as he pulled the blanket over the two of them…

She smiled, too.

And then she slept.

Matt didn't sleep.

There was no reason why he shouldn't. The tender was comfortable enough. Sure, his feet had to rest on the side but it was more comfortable than a bed on the rock-strewn sand. He did a bit of recreational hiking. He was used to sleeping rough.

Their problems had been solved. Rescue was on its way.

There was no reason at all why he should lie with Meg tucked into the crook of his arm and stare at the dark and think…

Meg.

He could understand why he should lie in the dark and think of the fire. But Meg?

It was the circumstances, he told himself.

But it was more than that. It was the sight of her at the wheel of the boat, handling the boat in the tricky seas as if she'd been born to it. Which obviously she had.

It was her insistence on seasickness pills. It was the way she'd persuaded Henry to treat Boof as a friend.

It was her competency and courage in the face of fire.

She'd saved them. That thought was overwhelming enough, but she'd done it with a warmth and empathy he could hardly comprehend. So many times since Amanda had died he'd felt helpless, and now this woman was making him feel even more as if there was an entire life skill set that had passed him by.

The way she looked. The way she smiled.

The way she felt…

Circumstances…

He was emotional, too, he told himself, and as she murmured in her sleep, as he instinctively held her closer, as he felt the warmth of her body against his chest he thought…

Circumstances?

He needed to get a grip because the way he was feeling, circumstances didn't come into it.

She woke in the small hours. Something must have woken her, but there was nothing but the hush of the waves against the sand and rocks in the sheltered cove.

The starlit night, the warmth, the peace…

And then she heard it, the faintest of whimpers.

She wiggled a little, so she could hold Henry. He'd been deeply asleep when Matt had lowered her into the tender and she'd been careful not to disturb him. Now, though… Matt's arm had been cradling her against him, forming a pillow. It took a wrench but she slid out of his hold and tugged the little boy to her.

'Hey, Henry, it's okay, we're here.' He was barely awake, maybe trapped in the same nightmare she'd had. But how much worse? His mother was dead. She was remembering the barren grief after her parents were killed, the fear, and all she could do was hold him.

'Matt's here, Boof's here and I'm here. And your grandma's waiting. She lit a fire on her cliff to say she's seen us. Hey, I wonder if she has a dog. And I bet she can fish, too, though if she can't, now you can teach her.' She was muttering inconsequential things, or maybe they were important. She wasn't sure he was hearing, but all that seemed important was to hold him close and let him know he was…loved?

Loved. That was the ingredient that was missing, she thought. She'd had her grandparents.

Did this little boy know that he was loved by someone?

'We've got you.' It was Matt's voice, firm, soft but inarguable. 'Meg and Boof and I are here for you, Henry. We're not going to let you go until we're sure your grandma will cuddle you. Sleep now.'

'You and Meg...' Henry's voice was a quavery whisper.

'And Boof and your grandma Peggy. We're a team. We're the caring-for-Henry team. Hey, Henry, how about we shift so we're a sandwich?'

And before Meg knew what Matt was about, he'd risen and lifted Henry over her, so the little boy was wedged between them.

'You're a Meg and Matt sandwich now,' Matt said sleepily, the suggestion inherent that this was simply part of a dream. A warm, safe, dream. And then, because the tender was very narrow—and because...okay, maybe he even missed the contact with Meg that she'd been valuing so much—his arm slid behind her head again, tugging her close. In the process it made a snuggly, warm V for one frightened child.

'Now,' Matt said firmly, 'everyone comfy? Everyone safe? Let's sleep again.'

Henry's sleep was almost instantaneous. Meg, though, lay and looked up at the stars.

'They're spectacular, aren't they?' Matt whispered. How *did* he know what she was thinking? 'You don't get these in New York. But, Meg, you need to sleep, too. You're as safe as Henry. I promise.'

Because this man was holding her?

It made no sense but that was the way she was feeling.

She hadn't liked him on first sight. Even on the boat, he'd responded to her attempts at conversation with the politeness of someone who moved in a rarefied atmosphere far from hers. She'd thought he was kind, but that kindness was overlaid with an arrogance that was almost innate. He'd thrown money at Charlie like water. He was accustomed to getting what he wanted from life, accustomed to getting his own way.

But he was holding her now and it felt…amazing.

She drifted back toward sleep but the feel of Matt, the thought of his words, his voice stayed with her.

It felt as if something had changed within her—and it felt wonderful.

CHAPTER SIX

RESCUE DIDN'T COME by helicopter. Instead, an hour after dawn, a cabin cruiser arrived. It was a boat that looked as if it had seen better days and those days were long behind it.

At the wheel was an elderly lady wearing men's trousers, an ancient fishing guernsey and huge black boots. Her hair was a mass of white curls, tied, incongruously, with a scarlet ribbon. She steered the boat expertly to within thirty yards of shore, cut the engine, tossed the anchor and hailed them.

There was no need to hail. They'd been watching her approach for the last fifteen minutes, Meg with growing incredulity.

This boat looked less seaworthy than *Bertha*. The skipper looked as if she was in her seventies. There was a dog standing at the bow—a dachshund, for heaven's sake.

This wasn't what Meg had hoped for.

Henry was beside her. She could hardly say, 'What on earth…'

She could think it, though, and as she saw how decrepit the boat looked she glanced at Matt and saw her dismay reflected.

Had Peggy decided to do the rescue herself?

'Ahoy.' Peggy's yell cut across the water. 'Is that a tender? Can you come and get me? Or just bring yourselves straight out. I can't get any closer because of the rocks.'

'Is anyone else coming?' Matt called.

'Just me.' Peggy sounded joyful. 'Henry, love, is that you?'

'Grandma.' Henry was on his feet. 'Grandma!'

'Yep, it's me and Stretchie. Stretchie—say g'day to Henry.'

And the little dog on the bow wagged her tail and gave an obedient woof.

The dog was cute, Meg conceded. And it was lovely to see Henry reacting with such joy to seeing Peggy. These were good points. But…

'That thing doesn't even look seaworthy,' Matt muttered, echoing her own dismay. Henry was out of earshot. He was standing on the shore, every fibre of his small being looking as if he needed to be out there hugging his grandma.

Matt and Meg were carting the tender to the water, but doubts were everywhere.

'Don't take Henry out.' That part seemed obvious. 'Matt, she might be planning to take Henry back to Garnett herself and leave us for the authorities to collect.'

'That's not happening,' Matt said grimly. 'I'm seeing him safe all the way. That's what I promised.'

Promised who? Meg thought. Promised Henry? She glanced across the cove at the little boy. His whole body language was joyful. His grandma had come to fetch him. He wouldn't be holding Matt to any promise.

But the knowledge came to her, sure and strong. This was a promise Matt had made to himself and Matt was a man who kept his promises.

It made her feel…solid. As if some things in life were right.

As if she'd found something good?

That was a dumb thing to think. Or maybe it wasn't, she conceded. Matt seemed honourable, dependable, caring. After a couple of days she'd never see him again, but it was good to know there were people like him in the world.

Except…after a couple of days…

Oh, cut it out. Just because he'd held her in the night... Just because he'd cared... This man was so far out of her orbit he might just as well belong to another species. Thinking about him... as she was thinking...

Fantasy.

'What's wrong?' he asked, and she hauled her head back to the here and now. To the sensible.

'Just worrying about Peggy.'

'It's okay. Even if she hasn't organised the authorities to come and get us, we'll use her radio to contact them ourselves.'

'It's not that.' She'd forced her mind to move from where her thoughts wanted to be—like centred around the guy at the other end of the boat—to where they should be. To an elderly woman taking her seven-year-old grandson to an island as remote as Garnett. She'd had qualms before. Now, looking at Peggy's rusty excuse for a boat, they surfaced again. 'It's just...'

'I know.' Once again she knew Matt got her thoughts. 'Meg, I have no control over this. I'm not family. I have no legal right to interfere. If I have any grave concerns, like the prospect of ill treatment or neglect, then I can contact the authorities, but you can see there's love between them. We can't interfere.'

'He's not going back to Garnett in that boat.'

'No,' Matt said with the same firmness she was feeling. 'I'll bring her to shore and then we all wait. How many muesli bars do we have left?'

'Enough, but we ate the chocolate ones for breakfast. We're down to bran.'

'Then let's get this organised fast,' Matt told her and then he smiled. 'Hey, Meg, cheer up. Peggy's the forerunner to rescue. If Peggy hasn't explained to the authorities that our situation is dire then we'll have to recontact. I want helicopters, skydivers, paratroopers, whatever it takes, but I'm a man who hasn't had coffee since yesterday. Things are indeed dire.'

It wasn't worth fixing the motor back onto the tender, so Matt rowed out. He used the excuse not to take Henry.

'You'll get in the way of my arms,' he told him. 'And I need room to bring your grandma to you.'

Meg stood at the shore and held Henry's hand. Henry clutched Teddy and waited.

Boof stood at Henry's other side. It was almost as if the big dog thought Henry was in need of protection.

Maybe he was.

Not from the little dog on Peggy's boat, though. The dachshund was greeting Matt with exuberance. Her body language was unmistakeable—*finally, something exciting's happening in my life.*

Just how isolated was Peggy?

Meg had heard of her—of course she had. Peggy had lived briefly at Rowan Bay before she'd bought the island, but that had been before Meg could remember. Peggy had been on her island for so long now that interest had faded.

Matt had climbed aboard. They were talking. A lot.

'Why are they taking so long?' Henry was jiggling at her side.

'I guess your grandma is showing Matt her boat.'

'But I want Grandma to see me.'

Finally Matt helped Peggy into the tender, handing her the dog. Peggy sat in the bow while Matt rowed, looking ahead at Henry, her eyes misty, her smile beatific.

Matt, not so much. His body language was… grim.

As the tender reached the cove Meg waded in and caught it. Peggy, though, was over the side, wading straight to Henry, catching him in her arms, holding him close.

'Oh, Henry.' Her voice broke on a sob and she buried her face in her grandson's hair. Henry clung right back.

And part of Meg relaxed. The biggest question—was Henry going to someone who loved him?—was being answered.

Matt had climbed out of the tender. He went to the stern. Meg was at the bow, preparing to lift the little craft yet again.

But Matt's face…

'What?' she said. Peggy and Henry were caught up in their hug. The dogs were sniffing each other. Meg and Matt could talk without anyone hearing.

'She doesn't have a radio.'

'On the boat?' Was he kidding? Who'd put to sea in Bass Strait without a radio?

'Worse than that,' Matt said. 'There's no radio on Garnett, either. It seems she's let her batteries run down and forgotten to reorder. She says the shock of her daughter's death made her forget everything, including that she'd swapped to backup batteries when the initial contact was made. My last contact with her kept dropping out and now I know why.'

'So she has no radio at all?' Meg stared across at Peggy in incredulity. 'To be on that island by herself with no way of contact...' Her mind was racing, not just to their immediate situation but to what lay ahead. 'Matt, if she can't be depended on to keep radio contact... To keep a child...'

'There's no use thinking that now,' he said roughly, and she knew his concern matched hers, maybe tenfold. 'But what to do?' He hesitated. 'Surely Charlie will try to contact you.'

'I'm surrounded by idiots,' she said bitterly. Frustration was threating to overwhelm her. She glowered up at him. 'Which hasn't been helped by hiring me to stay until you were sure Henry was settled. And offering Charlie that ridiculous amount on a daily basis. He'll be rubbing his hands with glee when I don't return. There's no way he'll be worrying.'

'You're blaming me?'

'It was ridiculous money.'

'But that's why you took the job.'

She glowered some more. The truth of his statement didn't help. 'I need a new roof,' she muttered.

'And I need security for Henry. So your justification is greater than my justification?'

'All right,' she threw at him. 'You're the hero and I've been a dope. Moving on...'

'You're not a dope. When we get back to Rowan Bay I'll personally organise you a new roof.'

Her eyes widened. 'You're kidding.'

'I'm not kidding.'

They'd been poised to carry the tender back up the beach. Now they were standing in shallow water, staring at each other from opposite ends of the boat.

'You don't even know how much a roof costs.'

'It doesn't matter.'

'Your offer of money got us into this mess in the first place.'

'My offer of money got Henry reunited with his grandma.' He motioned to Peggy, who was cradling Henry as if he was the most precious thing. 'You're saying that's a bad thing?'

'But you can't just buy me a new roof. Why should you?'

'Because I'm wealthy,' he told her. 'To be honest, Meg, I'm very wealthy. One roof, no matter how large, couldn't possibly dent my income. And you've been put to enormous inconvenience.'

'It's not my boat that sank. And I'm still being paid by the day, remember?'

'And those days might now stretch. Realistically, Meg, is there any way you'll be missed before Monday?'

'Maybe not,' she conceded. 'But Monday... I'll definitely be missed then. Charlie has a charter booked and I'm skippering. He'll have twelve angry corporates—it's a team-building fishing trip—demanding their money back. Also, I phoned Maureen, my next-door neighbour, before I left. She's feeding my chickens but by Monday she'll be asking questions.'

'So three days.' He stared across at Meg's bag. Oat-and-bran muesli bars. Not many.

He also looked at the water container they'd hauled from the tender. Four people and two dogs.

There was silence as they hauled the tender up the beach. Meg's mind was racing and, it seemed, so was Matt's.

'Mrs Lakey,' he called and Henry's grandma released her grandson—just to arm's length—and turned.

'Call me Peggy,' she said, and Meg could hear tears in her voice. 'Thank you for bringing me my grandson. And you put yourself in harm's way...'

'Our boat burned, Grandma,' Henry told her, sounding awed, and Peggy tugged him tight again.

'And I didn't even know. Last night I was terrified. If I hadn't seen your fires...'

'Peggy, do you have water on your boat?'

'I have a thermos,' she said, sounding confused. 'Half-full. It'll be cold now, though.'

'And that's all?'

'There's plenty of water on Garnett.' She didn't sound bothered. 'I guess your friends will send a boat for you soon enough. We should all go home and wait.'

Meg turned and stared out at Peggy's tub of a boat. So did Matt.

'It's a risk,' Meg said at last. 'But while this weather holds... I think we should attach the tender behind Peggy's boat and head to Garnett.'

'It doesn't even *look* seaworthy,' Matt muttered.

'I'll need to check the engine. And I mean really check. I want a couple of hours in the hull.'

'You know enough about engines to do that?'

'It's my splinter skill,' she told him. 'Holding old engines together with pieces of string. Mostly I win.'

'You didn't check *Bertha*.'

That brought a glower. 'Charlie assured me she'd been checked. You were in a rush. I was dumb enough to take his word.'

'Meg…'

'What are our choices?' she asked. 'Send Henry with Peggy without us? No way. Stay here? In three days we'll be seriously dehydrated. I'll check and double-check.'

'My boat's fine.' Peggy was listening, starting to look offended.

'She might seem fine,' Meg retorted, 'but look what happened to the *Titanic*. I'm checking.'

'She's checking,' Matt said, sounding bemused. 'There's a new order on this island. Rule of Meg.'

'Are you saying I'm bossy?' she demanded.

'I'm not saying you're bossy,' he told her. 'I'm saying you're awesome.'

Three hours later, filthy beyond belief, a greasy, oil-spattered Meg decreed the boat was as sound as she could make it.

'It hasn't been serviced for years,' Meg told Matt as they loaded the dogs into the tender.

Peggy and Henry were already aboard Peggy's boat. 'Matt, how can Peggy care for a child with this sort of attitude toward basic safety?'

'I'm starting to think she can't,' Matt said. 'But legally I have no choice but to take him to Garnett.'

'And if it turns out he's not safe?'

'There's a bridge we cross when we reach it.'

'Not a bridge,' she said grimly. 'Just a nasty piece of water known as Bass Strait.'

CHAPTER SEVEN

THEY MADE IT and Garnett Island was okay.

Garnett Island was safe.

The first few hours were busy: securing the boats, trying—and failing—to figure out a way to get the radio working, checking and using Peggy's pantry to make scratch meals—tinned spaghetti and sauce, and some herbs Meg found in Peggy's riot of a garden—chopping wood to get heat into the house, and coming to terms with the fact that Henry wouldn't be able to stay on the island. Safe or not.

After dinner Peggy tucked her grandson into his specially prepared bedroom and read him a story. Matt checked after half an hour and found the two of them asleep.

He left them there, huddled together, and came back to the kitchen to find Meg poking hopelessly at the woodstove.

'There's a hole in the flue,' she told him. 'There's no way it'll stay damped down overnight. I also suspect the chimney's blocked. Every time there's a gust of wind outside I get a back blast of smoke.'

'Peggy can hardly chop wood anyway. Meg, they can't stay.'

She wiped her hands on her truly disgusting jeans. She'd been dirty when he'd first met her, he remembered, just off an early-morning fishing charter. Since then she'd coped with a fire on the boat, taught Henry to fish, slept in her clothes and spent hours tinkering with the engine of Peggy's ancient boat. She'd had a wash when she got here but making the stove hot enough to heat dinner had undone what little improvement there'd been.

But she turned from the stove and looked at him thoughtfully, and once again came that almost ridiculous thought... *She's beautiful.*

'Want a walk on the beach?' she asked. She was smart as well as gorgeous, this woman. The message between them didn't need to be spoken—they needed to talk out of earshot of the two upstairs, and the old ceilings were thin and cracked.

So they walked down the track to the cove, where the boat was tied at Peggy's jetty.

The night was still and warm. The moon was

almost full. It was low tide. The wet sand was a shining ribbon. The place *looked* like paradise.

'We've been so lucky,' Meg said. They'd walked almost in silence until they'd reached the cove. Now, as he helped her down an incline where the sea had washed away steps, there was no need for silence, but still it seemed wrong to break the peace of this place. Meg's voice was almost a whisper, as if she agreed with him.

'Bass Strait's one of the wildest pieces of water in the world,' she told him. 'This jetty…' She motioned to the wooden structure where Peggy's boat was tied. 'It looks okay from the top but I checked when you were lifting Henry and the dogs off. The wood's rotting underneath. One big sea could smash it. Matt, the weather we've had over the last few days has been extraordinary. I need you to understand that.'

'Why?'

'Because you're thinking of all the reasons Peggy can't stay here and I'm adding another. Or more. The place is ramshackle. Peggy's supposed to get supplies once a fortnight but there'll be times when a boat can't land. If this jetty goes it'll be impossible. Her shopping list is on the fridge and it's all over the place. Items written three times. No fresh fruit. Despite having no backup batteries for the radio, she hasn't written them down. She's using solar power with battery storage, but even those batteries need replacing. And tonight, fixing dinner…she hardly seems to know what's in the pantry. I know her daughter's just died and she's stressed but this is survival stuff.'

'I get it,' he said heavily. She was saying nothing he hadn't already figured.

'I'm so glad you brought him yourself rather than sent him with a paid travel escort. To have dumped him here…it doesn't bear thinking of.'

'No.'

She glanced up at him, and then away, as if she didn't want to watch what was happening on his face. He didn't want to think about that. This situation was doing his head in.

'I made enquiries,' he said heavily. 'Peggy's not too old to take care of a grandchild. She owns the freehold of this island. She seemed to have regular suppliers. I asked about schooling and she had that nailed, too. School of the Air and occasional trips across to Rowan Bay to integrate with the kids there. She sounded competent, in charge…'

'And desperate to have her grandson,' Meg finished for him. 'There's no doubt she loves him.'

'And he, her. Have you seen that scrapbook? Every single week, a letter. You know, I should have twigged at that. Letters instead of emails. No internet. Intermittent telephone calls via her radio. I didn't ask enough questions.'

'But you came,' Meg said gently. 'You can hardly beat yourself up now.'

'So what the hell do I do?' It was almost a groan.

'Contact Social Services?' Meg was watching him, her expression thoughtful. 'After all, he's no business of yours.'

But it wasn't a statement. It was a question, and both of them knew it.

Henry was no business of his.

Meg was right, he wasn't. But for so many years…

'He sits in my office.' The words were almost an explosion, breaking the peace of the night. 'I remember the first time she brought him into work. He was four and she had a business lunch. "Sit there and don't bother anyone," she told him. I heard her as I passed on the way to a meeting. She told her secretary to keep an eye on him, but an hour later I found him sitting exactly where she'd left him, with two picture books and a computer game. He was watching neither, just staring ahead, trying not to cry. Luckily I had an understanding client. We all ended up making paper planes while we talked about the complexities of bitcoin transfer for a property settlement. But Amanda didn't get back for another hour and that was just the start of it. I almost sacked her, but I realised if she left my company then Henry would be in the same situation somewhere else. To be left like that...'

He broke off, appalled at the emotion in his voice. He hadn't realised quite how much he cared until right now.

Meg didn't comment. She was letting himself pull himself together, he realised. Giving him the space he needed.

They walked a bit more along the ribbon of sand. She was a peaceful woman, he decided. She hadn't jumped in with words of outrage. She hadn't even commented. And finally, when the next question came it was strangely out of left field.

'So tell me about you.'

'What...?'

'I'm hearing empathy,' she explained. 'You and Henry. Am I right?'

'That's got nothing to do with—'

'How you're feeling. I think it does. Did you ever get left like that?'

'My parents are wealthy.'

'Yeah, like that answers questions,' she said dryly. 'If Amanda was a lawyer in your firm then I imagine she didn't lack money, either. Money doesn't prevent loneliness. So, your childhood—'

'It's none of your business.'

'Of course it's not,' she said cordially. 'It's just, I'm feeling ties all over the place, emotion, need, empathy. I'm trying to sort it in my head.'

'I'm paying you to bring us to this island, not practise amateur psychology.'

'Ouch,' she said but she didn't sound offended. 'But you can't blame me. Social niceties are for others. I'm guessing you went to the best schools. Me, I left school when I was sixteen. It's a wonder I know how to use a knife and fork.'

She was smiling. Laughing at herself. Taking the tension out of the situation.

Making him smile?

His prickles settled. She was asking personal

questions. Two could play at that game—and he really wanted to know.

'So how come you left school at sixteen?' he asked. 'And don't tell me it's because you're dumb. I don't believe it.'

'How can you be smart with no education?'

He could hear a note of regret behind the light words. 'You were born smart.'

'Yeah,' she said dryly. 'Thanks, but...'

'But tell me. Why?'

'Because isolation sucks.'

It was a blunt answer, harsh even. They were walking slowly along the moonlit sand. They were looking out at the night-time seascape instead of each other.

It was a good time for revealing...all?

'You were lonely at school?' he asked cautiously.

'I loved school.'

'Then why...?'

'Because Grandma died.' She sniffed, almost defiantly biting back emotion. 'Okay, brief history. My grandpa was a fisherman and so were Mum and Dad. We shared a big old house up on the headland overlooking Rowan Bay. Big garden, enough land to run a few cows. Gran kept chooks. Her veggie garden was the best. Mum and Dad were sad they couldn't have any more kids after me, but I had the best childhood. I had four grown-ups who loved me. Then, when I was eleven, Mum and Dad were killed in a car crash and our world sort of folded. I was okay. I was still loved, but Dad was Gran and Grandpa's only child. Gran never got over it. She used to sit on the front porch and wait for them to come home, but of course they never did. And then she got cancer. She died the day after my six-teenth birthday and it was awful.'

'I'm so sorry.'

'Yeah, well, I was still…okay. I was a kid. I had mates in Rowan Bay. Life went on. But after Gran died, Grandpa started sitting, as well. He stopped going out in the boat. He just sat. And one day I came home from school and looked at him and I thought he's not even seeing me. I got the biggest fright. I suddenly thought, he'll get cancer, as well. I know it's illogical but I couldn't shake it.'

'So…' he said cautiously, seeing her as she'd been then—alone, terrified.

'So the next day I didn't go back to school. I made Grandpa take me out fishing and we fished ever since. And it worked. We were a great fishing team. We had fun. Then two years back, he got sick. I've spent most of the last couple of years looking after him. Which was expensive to say the least. I had to sell the boat but I didn't care. We were together all the time. He died six months ago and I don't regret a single moment of the time I had with him.'

She paused then, obviously regrouping, and she managed a smile. 'So if you ask me to say g'day in French or solve some sort of fancy equation I'm not your woman, but I can strip a mean engine and if you want a fish dinner I'll get it on the plate for you. So that's me, done. How about you?'

He didn't answer.

He felt winded.

And ashamed?

He was smart enough to read the gaps in her story. He was also smart enough to hear the loneliness. A kid with lost parents. A teenager dealing with an old man with what sounded like chronic depression and then terminal illness. A young woman putting her life on hold…

'Come on,' she urged as they kept walking. 'Your turn.' Amazingly she was back to being cheerful. 'Fair's fair.'

'Mine's boring in comparison.'

'So tell me.'

After that, he hardly had a choice.

'I was a lot luckier than you,' he told her. 'I'm an only child, too, but I had both parents and grandparents. My grandparents are gone now, and Dad died three years ago but for my childhood I had an intact family. My mother's still hosting society lunches, travelling, lording it over the ladies of Manhattan. She keeps in touch. I might be heir to the family dynasty but she sees herself as the McLellan matriarch. Even the most remote cousin knows its worth.'

Meg frowned, as if she was detecting undertones. As well she might. She was dissecting his words, looking for the parts she didn't understand.

'Family dynasty?'

'Historically a line of hereditary rulers.'

'I know that.' She glowered. 'I may not be educated but I'm not thick.'

'Sorry.'

'So you should be. So in the US... I figure the Kennedys are a dynasty. How does the description fit the McLellans?'

He smiled ruefully. She was smart, this woman. And...insightful? Seeing what was at the core of what he was saying. He took time to think of an answer that'd respect her.

'In Manhattan? A family succession playing a leading role in the financial world. My grandfather explained it to me when I was six. Our family has power.'

'So you rule Manhattan.'

'Not quite,' he said dryly. 'But we do have influence.'

'Hmm.' She cast him a thoughtful look, then moved on to the personal. 'So your mum and dad… They didn't live in the house you were telling me about?'

'My father was living in Sweden when he died. My mother hasn't been near McLellan Place for years.'

'They divorced?'

'They'd never have divorced. That doesn't mean they didn't have partners but partners came and went. They both…bored easily.'

She thought about that, too, and then cut straight to the bone. 'So did you bore them, as well?'

Ouch. What was he revealing?

'Maybe,' he said neutrally, trying not to feel as if she'd just nailed him, that she was seeing him as a kid alone apart from staff. His parents had indeed found parenthood too boring for words.

She walked a little way into the shallows,

kicking up water before her. She was still bare-footed—none of Peggy's shoes came close to fitting her.

She was giving him space.

'So this house in the Hamptons...' she said at last when the silence started to get oppressive. 'The cousins...family... You get together there for Christmas and stuff?'

'Not there. When my father died I bought the place from the estate so it's mine. I go there occasionally.'

'By yourself?' And then she caught herself and peeped a grin across at him. 'Whoops, sorry. I'm not inquiring about your legion of lovers.'

'So I shouldn't inquire about yours?'

She chuckled. 'I might even tell you.' She left the water and came up the beach to join him again. 'I've just knocked back one of the most romantic proposals you could imagine. Graham, Charlie's son, thinks I'll make a fine wife. He's seen me pulling an engine apart and putting it back together, and his passion's for expensive, stupid cars. He's eaten some of the cookies I bring into the office and he's seen me fish. He's also seen me clear a drain, chop wood and cart a drunken punter off the boat, all by myself. A woman who can cook, clean, gut a fish, keep his car on the road and put him to bed when he's drunk... I'm his wet dream. He says I can sell Grandpa's place, pay off his mortgage, plus the money he owes his ex-wife, and we can live happily ever after.'

'And yet you knocked him back?' he said faintly and she chuckled again. It was a great chuckle, soft and sexy.

'I know. I'm so fussy. Graham says I'm doomed to be an old maid.'

'I'm sure you're not.'

'I don't think I'd mind.' She paused, turning to stare out to sea. 'There are a lot worse things to be. To have a marriage like your parents'...'

'It suited them. They had money, the family name, the prestige of power.'

'Power?'

'Money means power,' he said simply. 'And there's a lot of money.'

'So this dynasty thing... When you offered to pay for my roof...'

'I suspect one day's power might more than pay for your roof.'

'And you have a lot of...power?'

'Yes. Financial juggling... It's in my blood.'

'Wow,' she said but strangely she didn't sound

impressed. She almost sounded sympathetic. 'But no one shares your house?'

But then she caught herself and the laughter returned. 'Sorry, I forgot. Your litany of lovers.'

'One a week and two on Sundays.'

'Now, why don't I believe that?'

Why? He didn't have a clue. She was starting to seriously unnerve him.

Or was *unnerve* the wrong word?

It was the setting, he thought. The place. The events of the last two days.

If he saw this woman in Manhattan he wouldn't look twice at her, he thought. He wouldn't even see her.

Or maybe he would. Grease stained, bare-footed, her short, copper curls tousled and stiff with salt and smoke… He'd glance twice.

Because she was out of place?

Because she was lovely.

'We'd best get back to the house.' He was starting to think he needed to be sensible where this woman was concerned.

'Yeah, we get to sleep on Peggy's living room floor.' She sighed. 'I'm thinking if we carted the tender up to the house it'd be more comfortable.'

'You can have the settee.'

'Have you sat on the settee?' she demanded. 'It has springs where no settee should have springs.'

'We'll manage,' he said and then, before he could stop himself, he reached out and took her hand. 'We've been through a lot together. Sleeping on a threadbare rug seems the least of it.'

'Yeah,' she said, but faintly, because suddenly she was looking down at their linked hands.

Because suddenly something was happening.

'Matt...' she said and her voice was uncertain.

'Meg.'

Meg. It was a name. A word. Why it hung...

Something indeed was changing.

The night was still. The beach was deserted. The sky was a glorious panorama of stars, the like of which he'd never seen before, making the night seem almost magic.

Which was pretty much how he was feeling now. Unreal. Time out of frame.

This woman was nothing to do with him, nothing to do with his world, and yet she was standing before him, looking up at him, her gaze a question.

And her question was the same as his.

And her chin tilted, just a little, as if her part of the question had been resolved. It was up to him...

And the night, the peace, the warmth…and, being truthful, his need, answered for him.

He cupped her face gently with his hands and drew her to him.

He kissed her.

What was she doing?

This guy had paid for her services. He was one of Charlie's punters. He was a customer, a fancy New York lawyer. He had absolutely nothing to do with her.

His hands cupped her face and she melted. Sense was nowhere.

His mouth touched hers and her willpower… everything…disintegrated in the need to be closer. His mouth claimed hers, and she felt as if her bones were melting. Her arms linked around him and it was as if she needed them to hold her up.

It didn't make sense but part of her was thinking she was merging. Becoming one? If she wasn't part of him she'd fall…

How stupid was that? But stupid was ignored. Everything was ignored. There was only the feel, the taste, the glorious wonder of being… cherished?

Loved.

There was a dumb word. She'd known this guy for less than two days. She was twenty-eight years old and she was sensible.

But sensible had gone the way of stupid. Irrelevant. The part of her brain doing the deciding decided the only available option was to concentrate on this kiss. To disappear into it, because it was magic.

She'd been kissed before—of course she had. She was twenty-eight years old and there'd even been some guys she'd seriously considered. A partner could have complicated her life with Grandpa but it wouldn't have made it impossible. She'd never ruled out falling in love.

But not one of the guys she'd dated had made her feel like this.

Desired. Beautiful. As if the cocoon she'd built around herself was shredding and what was emerging was someone she didn't know. She was someone who held this gorgeous, hunky, tender, strong, clever, amazing man close and who was claiming him.

Because that was what this kiss was. She wanted him, simple as that. Every fibre of her being was tuned to this overpowering need.

The kiss deepened and deepened again. His

hands tugged her hard against him and she knew his desire was as great as hers.

But maybe they weren't separate desires. Maybe they were the same, because that was how she was feeling. As if her body were fusing. One kiss…

It was so much more.

One body?

She loved the feel of him. His strength. The rough texture of his thick, dark hair as she ran her fingers through. The roughness of the stubble on his jaw. The sheer, arrant maleness of… Matt.

'Matt…'

And somehow, through the passion of the kiss, she heard herself say it. And she heard in her voice her desire, the release of every vestige of self-control.

And he heard it, too, and somehow, appallingly, it made a difference. She felt his body stiffen, just a little. Just enough to matter.

He broke away. His hands still held, but as he gazed down at her in the moonlight she saw shock.

It was enough to send the same sensation through her. She tugged away and he let her go. They were left staring at each other, disbelief reflected in both their eyes.

It was Matt who pulled himself together first. Who managed to speak.

'I don't suppose,' he said in a voice she hardly recognised, 'that when we jumped off our burning boat you thought about packing condoms?'

It was enough. It made her laugh, even if the laugh came out choked.

'I… No. I don't know what I was thinking. And what sort of emergency bag doesn't contain condoms?'

'It's a problem,' he said, gravely now. 'Though, Meg, maybe it's just as well.'

'Maybe it is.' She was still having trouble getting her voice to work. 'Matt, this situation is complicated enough. We do not need sex.'

'No?' And astonishingly there was laughter in his voice.

She looked up into those gorgeous eyes and found herself smiling in return. This situation was absurd. They'd been thrown together by the most appalling of circumstances. Emotion was everywhere.

Sex might even have been good.

Great?

'We both need to take cold showers,' she said, trying for astringency.

'Have you seen Peggy's hot-water service? That's exactly what's in store for us.'

She knew that. She'd had to heat water on the stove to give Henry a meagre bath.

Henry. The future.

'We both know he can't stay here.' She said it deliberately, not just because it was important but also because it took their minds—and their hands—off each other.

Laughter died.

'I know that,' he said. 'Okay, Meg O'Hara. Let's head back to the house and draw straws as to who gets to sleep on the lumpy settee or the hard floor. Reality starts now.'

It did.

But as they turned, Matt took her hand. Maybe it was because it was dark and she could trip on the rough track.

Maybe it was because he thought she needed protection.

Maybe it was because...they both wanted it?

Regardless, his hand held hers and she left it there. She even gripped his back.

It might be time for reality but she wouldn't mind fantasy for just a while longer.

* * *

Meg slept on the settee, buffered from broken springs by a quilt and exhaustion.

Matt tried to sleep on the floor. Since he was a kid and a friend's family had introduced him to hiking, he'd used camping, the wilderness to break the pressure of the stresses of the financial world. He was used to sleeping rough. A carpeted floor, cushions, quilts, didn't stop him sleeping.

Meg within arm's reach was a different proposition. He lay and stared into the dark and listened to her breathing and wondered what had just happened.

He'd kissed her.

He'd kissed women before. This was more than that. Much more.

It was the situation, he told himself. The emotion surrounding Amanda's death, Henry's bereavement. The long flight over here, jet lag, worry for Henry, then the fire on the boat and the adrenalin charge that had gone with it. The layers of sophisticated protection that he'd built around his emotions had been pierced and the kiss was the result. So it was the place, the situation.

The woman.

He lay and listened to her soft breathing and a part of him wanted to move across and take her into his arms. To feel her softness against his chest. To feel her mould against him, to need him…

Maybe that was it. The women he dated never needed him. He dated women who matched his world, sophisticated, intelligent…

Meg was intelligent.

And warm. And caring. And funny.

And the way she'd responded to his kiss…

Yeah, he wanted to be on that settee with her. Which was a joke. She was sleeping around broken springs as it was.

If he gathered her to him, if he said…what he wanted to say…how much more would be broken?

She was twenty-eight—old enough to protect herself, and old enough to know the rules in chance encounters. And yet the way she looked at him, the way she smiled, the sound of her chuckle…

She wasn't old enough. She wasn't savvy. If he took this further…

Did he want to?

For heaven's sake, he'd known her how long? What was he doing, thinking further?

He didn't do commitment. One day maybe? The McLellan billions demanded an heir and there were plenty of women in his orbit who knew how his world worked, who'd fit pretty much seamlessly into his life. But Meg...

What the hell was he thinking?

It was late. He was tired. What he was thinking was just plain stupid.

Close your eyes and go to sleep.

It wasn't about to happen.

CHAPTER EIGHT

THE NEXT DAY was so glorious Meg could imagine living on Garnett herself.

'But this weather won't hold,' she told Matt. 'Believe me.'

Peggy had taken her grandson fishing. They could see them down on the jetty, the white-haired grandma coaching her grandson as Meg had coached him the day before.

They'd gone off happily, although there'd been one dispute. 'You can't use barbed hooks, Grandma,' Henry had been explaining as they left. 'It hurts their mouths.'

That had made Meg smile. She'd turned to Matt, expecting to find him smiling as well, but instead she'd caught him looking at her. Just... looking.

He'd glanced away and made some innocuous remark about Henry's broadening education, but the expression she'd caught had her unsettled.

Henry was wearing one of Peggy's windcheaters, the sleeves rolled up, the hem hanging to his knees. He seemed cheerfully oblivious.

Meg and Matt had both decided their filthy jeans and trousers would have to keep on keeping on, but Matt's shirt and Meg's windcheater were currently flapping on the line. Meg was wearing one of Peggy's T-shirts, far too tight.

Matt was wearing...nothing at all.

Apart from his trousers, of course. Not that that helped. He was naked from the waist up.

Meg had tried not to watch as he'd chopped enough wood to keep them warm for a week. She'd failed. The sight of that naked chest, the delineation of muscles... A New York financier had no right to look like that.

And now... She'd been sitting on a log overlooking the cove, watching the pair below fish. Matt came and sat beside her and he brought his naked chest with him and she thought... She felt...

Like a sensible woman had no business thinking or feeling.

'So, plan,' he said, and she had to haul her thoughts away from an entirely inappropriate path and focus on... What had he said?

'Plan?'

'You know what I mean.'

She did. While Matt had chopped wood this morning she'd tried to distract herself by investigating the contents of Peggy's fridge and her pantry. The results had left her horrified.

'It's a wonder we survived last night's dinner,' she told him. 'There's stuff in that fridge that's about to walk out on its own.'

'You don't think it's the shock of losing her daughter, of trying to plan for Henry? Grief can make you fuzzy-headed.'

He got that, then. Impressive. This man was smart—that had never been in question. He was kind. He was also…empathetic?

'It can,' she agreed, thinking of the things her grandparents had done while in the throes of grief. 'But the pantry's full of weevils and she hasn't noticed. That's long-term.'

'Ugh.'

'And the battery thing… If I lived here, I'd have half a dozen sets of rechargeable batteries for extra solar storage and for the radio. If she were to get sick… If Henry was to fall and cut himself…'

'I know,' he said heavily. 'So where do we take it from here?'

'Let me talk to her.'

'You…'

'I'm good with oldies,' she said hesitantly. 'I could talk my grandpa into letting me help him shower. If I can do that, the next step's world peace.'

'But if she leaves the island...where do you propose they go?'

'Is that up to you and me to decide?' Meg asked. 'Matt, one thing I've learned from living with my grandparents is that age shouldn't take away choice. Yes, Peggy's struggling and maybe she might need help, but it's her life we're talking about. Seeing her this morning, watching Henry... I suspect we'll be pointing out stuff she already knows. She might even have a plan. Let's give her the respect of making a choice herself.'

Except Peggy didn't have a plan. They found that out after dinner. Fish caught by Henry, seared to perfection. Potato crisps made from potatoes Meg had dug from a neglected vegetable patch. A stir fry of greens from the same source.

Matt could have walked into the best restaurant in New York, eaten that meal and come out happy.

As soon as dinner was done, Henry crashed. He'd spent the day fishing, exploring the island with the dogs, doing stuff he'd never done in his life. He was exhausted.

Peggy also looked grey with fatigue, but she found enough energy to read him a bedtime story without going to sleep herself. Then she came down and sat at the kitchen table and faced them both. They all knew it was time for things to be brought into the open.

'I know what you're going to say,' she said heavily before either Matt or Meg could find space to comment. 'I can't keep him here. I hoped I could, but when the battery failed... It was my stupid fault, but it's a sign. I'm not as sharp as I should be. This was my lifestyle choice but I thought today, what if Henry gets something like appendicitis? When I heard Amanda was dead, the shock... Losing Amanda... All I wanted was to have him here. I know now it's impossible. I should have faced it before but I'm facing it now. So...' She looked helplessly at the pair of them. 'What do I do about it? Will you help me? Please?'

Matt flashed Meg a look. Peggy had known... His respect for Meg was increasing by the moment, but her face didn't show for an instant that she was satisfied with her call. Her face was pure concern.

But she left it for him to speak first.

'Peggy, we're sorry,' he said. 'But if you can't keep Henry here…do you want to be evacuated with him?'

'Yes.' There was no hesitation. 'You know Amanda's father was American? I was born on a farm south of Rowan Bay. Amanda was the result of my one stint at trying to be a city girl. I even ended up with American citizenship, but look where that left me. Both Amanda and her father despised the lifestyle I longed for. Finally, I had to walk away and I've been a loner ever since.' There was a wealth of sadness in her voice, a wealth of regret.

She sighed and looked around at the peeling paintwork, at the obvious signs of neglect. 'I've loved this island but now I can't even afford to fix the house. I'll need to find somewhere to rent in Rowan Bay, though what with… It'll take time to sell this place even if I can find a buyer. No one wants rocky outcrops in such a climate. And I can't… I can't…'

She stopped. A tear rolled down her wind-weathered cheek and Meg reached out and took her hand.

'Hey, Peggy, don't cry. Let's take one step at a time. What we need is a plan.'

'A plan…' Peggy looked at her as if such a thing was unthinkable.

'A plan,' Meg said firmly. 'Something to give us breathing space.'

We? Matt thought blankly. *Us?* He'd hired Meg to skipper a boat. What was she doing, offering to be in the mix?

But the *we* was continuing. 'Why don't we spend tomorrow packing?' she suggested. 'We can pack essentials and things like Stretchie's favourite ball, your favourite pillow, your best fishing rod. Precious stuff we can take with us when we're evacuated. When you're settled, I can bring you back in one of our bigger boats and we'll collect the rest.'

'But where will we go?' Peggy's voice was muffled, grief mixed with despair.

And Meg's grip on her hand tightened. 'I've been thinking of that, too,' she said. 'I have a big old house on the headland south of Rowan Bay. I've lived there with my grandparents but sadly now I'm on my own. So I have four bedrooms, lots of squishy old furniture, lots of space. It's not grand but it's comfy. I have a huge garden—well, it used to be a garden, now it's sort of wilderness because I don't have time to care for it. I have chooks. I have five acres of coastline where you can fish or walk or just get to know your grandson. Peggy, you're very welcome to come and stay with me for as long as you want. While you get your breath back. While you plan. It sounds sensible to me but what about you? What do you say?'

It obviously took Peggy's breath away. She didn't answer, just stared at Meg, astounded.

It pretty much took Matt's breath away, too. He'd been ready to swing into action, find them a hotel until he could organise a rental property, foot the bill himself. He opened his mouth to say it—but then he closed it again.

He was due back in the States. He had massive financial contracts hanging on his return. He'd spent a lot of today worrying that he couldn't simply dump Peggy and Henry and leave.

But now, with one extraordinary offer, the responsibility had been lifted from his shoulders. By one extraordinary woman.

'But…' Peggy was gazing wide-eyed at Meg, as if she couldn't believe what she was hearing. 'But for how long?'

'For as long as you want,' Meg said soundly. 'To be honest, my place is lonely. Boof will love company and so will I. How are you at gardening?'

'I love gardening. I've struggled to keep this one going but if I had a bit of help...'

'There you are, then,' she said, smiling. 'I spend my days skippering charter boats and my garden's rubbish. We'll fix it together. If you can push a mower and pull weeds, there's your rent taken care of. And Henry can go to the local school. I imagine it'll take him time to settle but it's a good school.'

She really was talking long-term. Matt was growing more and more astounded.

'Meg...' he started and she flashed him a warning look.

'You have any objection to our plan?'

And there it was again. *Our.* She'd incorporated herself into this situation, she'd taken responsibility, she was one of them.

One of...*us*?

No. Because suddenly he was the outsider. He was the one going back to the States while Meg took over.

That should be fine. He couldn't think of a better solution. He wasn't convinced Peggy's confusion was solely down to grief and shock, but Meg would be there, keeping an eye on them both. Caring.

And then he thought, why did that make him feel empty? Bereft?

There was no reason. After all, Henry was the child of an employee, nothing more. The problem of what to do with him had been solved. He could head back to the States, conscience clear.

'There will be some money coming through from Amanda's estate,' he said, deciding to go down the professional route. The much less emotional path. 'Not as much as you might expect. To be honest, she seems to have led a fairly flamboyant lifestyle.' He'd been at her apartment, a penthouse overlooking Manhattan. He'd seen the wardrobe overflowing with shoes even he recognised as extraordinary. 'But there will be enough for you to rent for a while once we find you a place.'

'I'd rather stay with Meg,' Peggy said, casting him a scared look. Like a child about to have a treat snatched away.

'You could put Amanda's money into trust for Henry,' Meg suggested. 'When Peggy sells the island, we can make a decision whether living with me is working. She can buy her own place then if she wants.'

'Meg, do you realise…?'

And he got a flash of anger. A look that definitely said, *Butt out.*

'I think it's a good plan,' she said. 'No, I think it's a great plan. I get a free gardener. Boof and Stretchie will have each other and so will Peggy and Henry. And me… I'll get to come home after a day's charter and the lights will be on. It'll be home again. Any objections, Matt McLellan?'

Any objections? Strangely the biggest was that he wasn't included. That was dumb. He really did need to get back. But before he realised what he was about to say…he said it.

'Can you put me up for a few days, as well? I need to assure myself that Henry's safe.'

'Henry will be safe,' Peggy growled. 'I'm not a total incompetent.'

'Neither am I,' Meg said, and astonishingly she grinned. 'But let's humour him, shall we, Peggy? Blokes like to be in charge and I suspect someone like Matt McLellan likes that even more than most blokes. So let's give him the illusion of control. It's a very good plan, Matt McLellan, but you're welcome to come stay in my house and see for yourself.'

And then she hesitated, appearing to think about what to say next.

'But Peggy and Henry's invitation is open-ended,' she told him when she'd thought about it. 'Yours is a few days only. I have a big house but it still doesn't feel big enough for the two of us. And now... I don't know about you two, but it's time I hit the sack. We have a heap of packing to do tomorrow, Peggy, and we have a plan.' Her grin returned. 'I do love a plan, don't you?'

She lay on the decrepit settee.

He lay on the floor.

It was barely ten o'clock. He never went to bed before midnight.

How could he sleep?

Meg's breathing was soft and regular. She was within arm's reach.

She was...

Meg.

He was starting to feel as if he'd never met a woman like this. A woman who faced the problems of the world and embraced them, solved them her way, without a thought to consequences.

Peggy was elderly and confused. Henry was seven years old and needy. She'd taken them under her wing as if such a commitment were no more than inviting house guests for a couple of days.

She knew it was more than that. He'd seen it in the look of defiance she'd flashed at him, like butt out, this is none of your business.

Peggy needed support. Henry needed love.

Once ensconced in Meg's house, could she ever ask them to leave?

Was she planning to?

'This is my responsibility.' To his horror he heard himself say the words out loud. What was he doing, talking to himself? And Meg heard. She stirred and rolled over to face him. The moonlight was streaming in the window and he could see the mound of her on the settee. A small mound. A power-packed mound.

A mound of decision, of warmth and of kindness.

Also profanity. She hit a broken spring as she rolled and her expression was pure sailor.

'Where's a pair of wire clippers when you need them?' she said bitterly. 'I went looking for them today and the only ones Peggy has are rusted closed. Now... What did you say?'

'I didn't.'

'Yes, you did. If I'm right... This is your responsibility? How so?'

'I never in a million years wanted to land them on you.'

'You didn't. Amanda's death did. You and I were simply conduits to get Henry to Peggy. You go home. I get to share my too-big house. Problem solved. Yikes, there's another b...'

He grinned. Her lightness was infectious.

But she'd almost scuttled to bed when Peggy retired and now... He had a feeling her swearing was out of character. Was she purposely reminding him of the gulf between them?

He didn't want a gulf, and right now even six feet felt like a gulf.

'You know, if we hauled your quilt and cushions onto the floor we could have one half-comfortable bed between us,' he ventured.

'Matt, I've checked Peggy's bathroom cabinet. There are no condoms there, either.'

'I didn't mean...'

'Yeah, you did. Or if you didn't it'd occur to one or other of us sooner or later. Probably sooner. And neither of us want...'

'I suspect that's the problem,' he said. 'Both of us want.'

'Then neither of us can have,' she said firmly. 'I'm heading back to my life running fishing charters from Rowan Bay. You're heading back to your life as a billionaire or whatever you are in Manhattan. Are you a billionaire, by the way?'

He had to tell the truth. 'Yes, I am.'

'There you go.' There was not the least hint of resentment in her voice. 'Poles apart. So you're heading back to your life, and you're not taking my broken heart with you.'

There was a big statement. 'Would it be broken?' he asked, cautiously, and he heard her gasp as she realised what she'd said.

'I… No. Of course not. We've known each other two days. But there is this…thing between us and if it gets any stronger…'

He got that, too. He didn't understand it but it left him wanting.

He wanted this woman.

She was being sensible. He had to be, too.

'You're stuck with the springs, then.'

'I can cope.'

'Meg, the money side…'

'Yeah?'

'There'll be all sorts of costs involved in having Peggy and Henry. I already promised you a new roof. Whatever else you need…'

'You want to pay?'

'Of course I do.'

'Okay, then,' she said, as if it didn't matter one way or another. 'If you really are rich and you really want…'

He did want, but it was more than helping out financially. He wanted to be involved.

But he wasn't needed. There was no place for him in this scheme and why that made him feel bereft…

It was too strong a word, he thought. He wasn't bereft.

Suddenly Meg's words came back to him.

I'll get to come home after a day's charter and the lights will be on. It'll be home again.

He found himself thinking… To come home from work late at night and find the lights on… To have this woman waiting for him…

Fantasy.

'Goodnight, Matt,' Meg said firmly and rolled over on her springs and swore again. 'I think we have things sorted. Sleep.'

Right. How was a man to sleep after that?

Things didn't feel sorted at all.

CHAPTER NINE

TWO DAYS LATER they came, in a helicopter, with all the bells and whistles a small boy could possibly require. It said a lot for the security Henry was now feeling that he could hold Matt's hand and watch the chopper land with fascination. And when the guy in charge, a yellow-jacketed member of the state's emergency services, walked across to the chopper to meet them, smiling his relief, saying, 'Well, are we pleased to see you! What happened to your boat?' Matt was stunned to hear Henry answer.

'It got burned,' he said, almost proudly. 'Meg tried to put it out but she coughed and coughed and then we had to get into the little boat and we were stuck on an island that was all rocks. Meg and me caught a fish and then Grandma came to find us. Only her radio's busted and Meg says everyone will be worried but you don't have to worry because Meg and Matt and Grandma and Stretchie and Boof looked after me.'

It was the most words Matt had ever heard Henry say. He found himself grinning, and his grin was matched by the guy in the yellow jacket's. Relief all round.

They'd all come out of the house as they'd heard the chopper. They were grouped together. Mum and Dad and Grandma and kid? For some reason that was what it felt like. Family. His pride in Henry seemed almost as deep as if the kid were his own.

He glanced at Meg and saw a shimmer of tears in her eyes. She was feeling the same?

'Got it in one,' the guy was saying in satisfaction and he went straight to Henry and gripped his hand. Henry shook it without blinking. 'I wish all our rescues were as straightforward. Well, young man, how can we help? Was anyone burned? No one injured at all?'

'Meg still coughs a bit,' Henry volunteered.

'She was in the cabin when the boat caught fire,' Matt said. 'She copped a fair dose of smoke inhalation.'

'I'm better,' Meg said and the guy nodded. He'd been joined by a couple of teammates now, all looking just as pleased. A boat missing at sea, especially with a child on board, was everyone's nightmare.

'We'll get our doc to check you out as soon as we reach the mainland,' the guy said. 'How about the rest of you? You need evacuation?'

And it was up to Peggy. She took a deep breath, took a firm hold of Henry's hand and nodded.

'Yes, young man, we do,' she said. 'I can't… We can't stay here any longer.' She cast a quick, fearful look at the helicopter and then looked deliberately down at Henry. 'How…how long does it take to get to Rowan Bay?'

'Less than half an hour, ma'am,' the guy said, gentling as if he sensed her fear. 'You'll be safe as houses.'

Safe. It was a good word. No, it was a great word and Peggy responded. She exhaled, all her fear of flying, all her love for her grandson combined in one long sigh.

'Then I can do it,' she managed. 'If Henry holds my hand all the way. Thank you, sir. Yes, please. Can you take all of us?'

What followed was a chopper ride that Peggy managed, eyes squeezed shut, Meg gripping one hand, Henry the other.

Henry, though, enjoyed the flight immensely. Life was suddenly an adventure. He coped okay with the reception at the little Rowan Bay airport. He became quiet again—some things didn't change—while official questions were asked, while the emergency services doctor took Meg into the office and did a fast examination, while the dogs checked out the little-used airstrip for rabbits. But he still seemed deeply contented.

Finally, Meg emerged, smiling. 'The doc says I need to take steroids for a few days until my lungs are clear,' she told Matt and Peggy. 'But I'm fine. The guys have organised taxis. Are we ready to go home?'

Home. It was a strange concept.

Matt had never felt less at 'home' in his life.

They made a fast stop at the general store and the pharmacy on the way. Matt and Henry needed pretty much everything, but half an hour later, armed with packages of new clothes, they reached Meg's place.

The house looked almost as ramshackle as Peggy's. Maybe not quite, Matt conceded. It was old and in need of paint. It definitely needed a new roof, but it wasn't actively falling down. With ancient settees on the wide veranda, a decent veggie patch, even if the rest of the garden looked in serious need of attention, and a view right out over the bay, it looked warmly welcoming.

A middle-aged woman, plump, aproned, beaming, came out of the front door to meet them.

'Meg,' she said in satisfaction. 'I knew there was something wrong. You should have heard what I said to Charlie when I realised he hadn't been in radio contact. I think the safety authorities will be having words. I was never more glad of anything when word came through you were safe. Your chooks are fine. You have a fridge full of eggs. I've just been in and put a casserole and apple pie in the oven. Now, who's this?'

Maureen was introduced to them all. She greeted Peggy and Henry with warmth but she eyed Matt with caution.

As well she might, Matt thought. He hadn't seen a razor for days and his new clothes were still in their wrapping. To say he was unkempt was an understatement. But with the way this woman looked at him came the odd, irrelevant thought. He was the one in this picture who didn't belong.

And maybe that was right. His job was done. He could organise a car to take him to Melbourne Airport, get on a plane and be back in the States tomorrow.

But he'd asked to stay and Meg had agreed. Didn't he have a responsibility to Henry?

Henry no longer needed him.

He couldn't just land this all on Meg and walk away.

But Meg was practically bouncing, showing them inside, opening bedroom doors, hauling open a linen cupboard and distributing sheets, filling water bowls for dogs, showing Henry where the dog toys were kept.

Peggy and Henry were happily following. So was Matt, but as he followed his feeling of dislocation deepened—as well as thinking he'd landed Meg with a life-changing set of circumstances and she'd taken them on as if it were nothing.

She was amazing.

'Lunch first and then I bags first bath,' she said. 'Peggy, is everything fine?'

'Everything's great,' Peggy said. 'Oh, Meg, if you're sure…'

'I'm sure,' Meg told her. 'This'll be fun.'

Fun. Once again Matt felt…hornswoggled.

And as if he had no place here and it mattered.

* * *

Back in the land of telecommunications, his phone was crammed with messages. Of course. He'd abandoned complex negotiations to bring Henry to Australia, and his world hadn't stopped because of it.

When he finally had time to check, it was four in the afternoon, which was midnight New York time. It was hardly the time to return business calls.

There was, though, one caller whose need for a response seemed more urgent than the rest. Helen, his personal secretary for years, was intelligent, competent and unflappable. But now she sounded…flapped.

She'd left ten different voicemail messages at various times over the last few days, each increasingly pressing.

'Matt, you need to ring me. Please, Matt, this can't wait. I need to speak to you, now.'

If it was anyone but Helen, he wouldn't ring at this hour but he could hear the increasing worry. For him to be out of range for this long was unthinkable. It was a wonder she hadn't organised a search party herself.

She answered on the second ring. He imagined her in her neat New York apartment, cool, collected, part of his ordered business world, but there was nothing ordered about the way she answered. 'Where the hell have you been?'

He explained but she hardly listened.

'Well, thank heaven you're okay,' she said, interjecting over his last words. 'But, Matt... something's happened. We've located Henry's father. Steven Walker. You know you asked me to keep looking? After you left I thought of searching through Amanda's client files from eight years ago, just on a hunch. And there he was. Of course, I wasn't sure—how many Steven Walkers do you think there are in the States? But on the off chance I took the liberty of ringing, ostensibly to let him know his lawyer had died and to check there was nothing outstanding we needed to cover. And at the end... I ventured. I sort of casually dropped that Amanda had a seven-year-old son. Matt, there was a silence on the end of the phone, almost like he expected what was coming. So I went for it. I said the father's name on the birth certificate was Steven Walker and we hadn't been able to find him. Could that possibly be him?'

And then Helen hesitated, seeming to gather herself for what needed to be said next.

'And then he said yes, it could. He was almost

cool about it, maybe as if he'd suspected. He asked what was happening with Henry. I told him and he thanked me and disconnected. He went away and obviously did some investigation. A few hours later he phoned back. He has a family of his own—actually children from three marriages. He says he'll want a DNA test but as long as that proves positive he'll accept responsibility.'

'That's…good,' Matt said cautiously.

'Maybe,' Helen told him. 'But there's more. He says it depends on the DNA result, but if it's positive…he says he's damned if he's letting a son of his live on some forsaken island in the middle of nowhere. He's wealthy. He sounds sensible but he also sounds tough. He says he'll provide housing, a nanny, "anything the kid needs", but he has to come home. Matt, I've done some preliminary investigation and checked with a couple of the other lawyers here. As the named father, he'll have priority over Henry's grandmother, even if there is a custody dispute. I don't know where that leaves you, Matt, but the lawyers in the office say you'll need to bring Henry back.'

Henry fell asleep before he finished his apple pie. He'd had a huge day. He had his grandma and his teddy, he had the dogs and he had Matt. Life was okay. Did Matt realise just how much Henry adored him? Meg wondered as Matt lifted the little boy and carried him to his bedroom.

And did Matt know how much he'd become attached to Henry? She'd watched him watching the child and she thought, for all his talk of detachment, the bond tied both ways.

And Peggy was bonded with Henry, too. She was exhausted, she'd coped with a helicopter flight that had clearly terrified her, but she'd spent the remainder of the afternoon making sure Henry was happy. She'd abandoned her beloved island for him. She was sitting cradling her mug of tea now, but the look on her face was almost peaceful. Her grandson was safe.

There was no doubt Henry was loved.

And then Matt returned and Meg glanced at his face and saw there was more to come. He'd seemed preoccupied since he'd made his phone calls. He'd asked to use her computer, the internet, and he'd locked himself in her messy excuse for a study until dinner time. She'd thought, of course, he'd have to catch up on business.

Now, though…she turned from the sink and saw his face and knew it was more than business.

'I need to talk to you both,' he said, and she

glanced at Peggy and saw the elderly woman brace. As if she, too, knew instinctively that something bad was coming.

Meg poured more tea for them all, slowly, sensing somehow they needed space for what was coming. And then they all sat down at her battered wooden table and Matt told them what Helen had told him. And what he'd learned.

He'd made the call to Steven Walker. Yes, he'd rung him at one in the morning but, dammit, this was his son.This was his kid's life. So he'd rung and found Steven had been doing his own investigation. He'd researched where Henry had been taken and he'd been horrified. He'd faced the options, he'd accepted responsibility and he'd made a decision.

'He doesn't necessarily want custody,' he told them. 'Although he'll accept it if necessary. He has kids from three relationships. He hardly wants more, but he sounds inherently decent. He had a relationship with Amanda that lasted for six months and then she broke it off and demanded he find himself another investment lawyer. He said she broke it off so abruptly he wondered why, and now he thinks maybe he was used. He's pretty angry about it but if the

DNA test proves positive he wants Henry back in the US.'

'But—' Peggy was staring at him, appalled '—Henry doesn't even know him. He doesn't even know he exists.'

'That's not Steven's fault,' Matt said gently. 'Peggy, he sounds reasonable.'

'It's not reasonable to take him away from me.'

'Henry's an American citizen with an American father,' Matt told her. 'Steven says if he'd known about him he would have interjected well before this. I'm sorry, Peggy, but he says he'll apply to the courts if necessary. If the DNA test proves positive—and he believes it will—then Henry has to come home.'

'To live with him?'

'He doesn't necessarily want that, although he'll provide it if necessary. He'll provide accommodation, a nanny, boarding-school fees...'

'No!' Meg spoke before she could stop herself. 'He's better off here. With his gran. With me.'

'I don't think that can happen,' Matt said, still gently. 'Steven's named on the birth certificate. Henry hasn't been living with Peggy so there's no established alternative. That Amanda didn't tell him of Henry's existence doesn't make a difference to his rights now. We need to face it.

I believe I'll have to take him back. Peggy, you might be able to persuade him to let you keep custody, but that argument will have to happen over there.'

Peggy's face was ashen. 'I won't let Henry go. I can't. And there's nowhere in the States I can go.'

'I've thought of that, too.'

Meg stared at him. His voice was calm, controlled, the complete opposite to the panic both she and Peggy were feeling. He'd had hours to think this through, she thought. He'd come to terms with it, and Henry was a colleague's child, nothing more. He was nothing to do with him.

And then she thought of the look on his face when he'd lifted a sleepy Henry and carried him to his bed. She thought, *No, Henry's much more.*

And his next words confirmed it.

'I have a plan,' he said, and she saw Peggy's look of despair take a tiny step back.

'A plan... So I can keep him.'

'I know you love him,' Matt said. 'And I also know you're an American citizen, as well. Your marriage gave you that. Steven's talking about setting up a home with a nanny, so why don't we simply arrange that for him? Make it easy for him to agree? What I'm proposing is that

you swap Meg's beachside home for my beachside home.'

Peggy stared at him, wildly. 'What…? What…?'

And Meg thought, *What is he saying?*

'It's not so different,' Matt said, calmly now,
as if he were talking about choices for what was
for dinner. 'Meg offered you a home with her,
and you accepted.'

'I want to live here,' Peggy said almost defiantly. 'We could be happy here.'

'And you could be happy at my house in the
Hamptons. It's big, it has a great garden and it's
right on the beach. There's a community there
Henry could be part of. You've been on an island for years so you'd be less isolated there than
you have been, but you could still have your privacy. There's fishing, boating, the ocean. I work
in the city but I could come down at weekends
to make sure things are okay, and yes, to see
Henry because, to be honest, I've grown fond of
him. His father could see him, too. And, Peggy,
once you're in the States…the custody thing…
Henry's kept all the letters you've ever sent him.
He'll tell any court that you've rung him, that
you've written, that you've been in contact with
him all his life. If he's living safely in the States
with his grandma, with me, I doubt Steven will

even fight you for it. What he's doing is what he thinks is the right thing for a child he feels responsible for. Let's make it easy for him. Come and live with me.'

'You won't be there.' She seemed…gobsmacked. Too much was happening, too fast.

'I'll be in Manhattan working but I can be there often at weekends. And I'll always be in touch. I can be with you in a couple of hours if you need me.'

'But I don't know anything about you.' Once more Peggy's voice rose in a wail. 'I know nothing about this place you say we could live in. How do I know…anything?'

'Come and see.'

'I won't fly.' The panic in her voice was real and dreadful. 'Not again. Half an hour was awful. How can I do more? I can't take him. I won't.'

'Peggy, slow down and think.' Matt's voice seemed like that of someone accustomed to providing reason in the midst of crisis. 'My house can provide you with a wonderful beachside place to live, with as much privacy as you want, with the fishing and beachcombing you love and, most of all, with a solid, secure home for you and for Henry. Is there any reason why my home's any less of an option than Meg's?'

'But I know Rowan Bay,' Peggy wailed. 'And I know Meg. At least… I knew her grandmother. I'm going on trust.'

'Then I'm asking for you to trust me. For Henry's sake.'

Peggy was crying now, tears slipping down her wrinkled face. It was so unfair to land this on her. 'I can't. I won't fly. I won't.'

'Peggy, you don't need to fly tomorrow,' he said. 'Henry's been through enough and this isn't urgent. We need to get the DNA sorted and, as I said, Steven's reasonable. He's relieved Henry's off the island and he'll give us time. But I believe we need to face the fact that there's little choice.'

'There is,' Peggy said wildly, and she turned to Meg. 'You go.'

'What?' Meg stared at her, taken aback.

'I shouldn't ask you,' Peggy said. 'After all you've done for us. But I know you, or I feel like I know you. You're a Rowan Bay girl. You're a loner, the same as me. You love the sea and dogs and I know you care for Henry. I can see it. So you go. Go back with him. I'll stay here, care for Henry, let us both get our breath back. You go to this place he's talking about. If you think it's a place Henry and I can live then I'll… I'll get on a boat. There must be ships that'll take us there.'

'I can't move to America,' Meg said, stunned.

'I'm not asking you to,' Peggy said, swiping away tears, and Meg saw a hint of stubbornness, the inexorable strength that had let her live on a solitary island for all these years. 'You check it out and come back and tell me. If it's really, truly okay, then we can go.' She blinked away the rest of her tears and suddenly looked hopeful. 'Is that a plan? Meg? Would that work?'

She was going to America.

How had that happened?

Fast, that was how. She'd seen Peggy backed into a corner and she'd promised. Now Matt was on the internet, emailing Steven, and she was sitting on the deck overlooking the bay thinking what had she done?

The door opened behind her. She heard Matt's footsteps.

She didn't look up.

'Can I have half a step?'

She moved over, but grudgingly, not the least bit sure she wanted him sitting beside her.

She needed time to work things out. To figure what exactly she'd promised.

'Done,' he said gently and she flinched. Done what?

'You want to tell me?'

He cast her an amused glance. 'You think I'm being bossy?'

'You and Peggy... Organising my life... Yes, I think you're being bossy.'

'Everything's tentative,' he said. 'I've made plans but they can be changed if you want to pull out.'

'Like I can pull out. I'm heading to the States to do what? A real estate inspection?'

'You promised Peggy,' he said gently. 'I'll cover all costs. I'll make it right with Charlie, and, let's face it, it'll be a sight easier than having Peggy and Henry living with you for years.'

She turned to him then, incredulous. 'Is that what you think? That I want to be rid of them?'

'They're strangers.'

'They need me.'

'They're not your family.'

'No, but they could be.' And then she heard what she'd said. She heard the raw need that had suddenly surfaced and she bit her lip and turned away.

'Is that what you want?' Matt said, sounding puzzled. 'Family?'

'I wouldn't mind.' Why not say it? This house had echoed with emptiness since Grandpa had died. Even though her offer might have seemed generous, there'd been a part of her that had thought living with Peggy and her grandson might even be fun.

And he'd heard it. She could see it on his face. The porch light combined with the moonlight let her see him as clearly as he saw her. It let her see the gravity of his expression, those intelligent, searching eyes that seemed to see…more than she'd let on.

But did he see, she wondered, just how confined her circumstances had made her? A lifetime of caring had her trapped in a job, in a lifestyle she'd had no choice in. At twenty-eight, she'd spent her life fishing and caring, hardly moving from the confines of Rowan Bay. Now, deep in debt, she had little choice but to continue that lifestyle. She could clear her debt—just—by selling the house, but where did that leave her? She'd have nowhere to live, no career.

To have Peggy and Henry live with her… To have someone to come home to…

Oh, for heaven's sake, that made her feel

needy. And vulnerable. She was neither of those things. She was tough as old boots. She'd heard Charlie describe her as such and she fought for that now. Meg O'Hara, the tough one.

But maybe Matt was seeing under the surface. Maybe he guessed.

'So here's a proposition,' he told her. 'While I've been on the phone to Steven I've been turning things over, looking at problems, searching for solutions. And, Meg, it might seem crazy but I have another proposition.'

'What?' It was hardly a graceful or grateful response but it was all she could come up with.

'Let's do what Peggy suggests,' he said. 'As soon as the DNA connection's confirmed, as soon as your cough's settled, let's you and me get on a plane and head back to the States. You can check out the house, look at it from all angles, think about it. But, Meg, maybe you could also look at it for you, too. Peggy's just a little bit…vague…and in a strange setting it might be worse. I'd like someone to take care of them. That person could be you.'

'Me…'

'They won't need all that much care,' he said hastily, as if trying to explain before she could refuse. 'Henry will be at school and Peggy will want to be independent. But it's a great place to live. If you wanted…there are charter companies down there, a lot less dodgy than Charlie's. You could get work with them. You could garden. You could fish. You could…' He hesitated. 'You could love Henry.'

'So you wouldn't have to?' It was out before she could stop it.

'I do love Henry.' He paused for a long moment and when he spoke again his voice had changed. 'I didn't know it for a while, but finally I'm starting to figure it out. Meg, my childhood's been bleak, solitary, not quite as bad as Henry's but almost. I don't…get close to people. I thought I was bringing him here to do him a favour but he's been sitting in the corner of my office for years. He's become… Yeah, I concede, he's become part of my life. Today, on the chopper coming back here, I watched his face, I could see the excitement. I could see the transformation. And I looked around and saw you watching him. Caring for him. I saw Peggy overcoming her terror of flying to be with him. And then I thought, you know what, I want to be in that equation, too. To love a kid… Surely that's a privilege.'

'I guess it is.' Her words were a bit shaky. Wary. She wasn't sure where this was going.

'And then I talked to Steven. His response was guarded but it was definite. If this was his kid then he was ready to do whatever it took to keep him safe. But then I thought, I hate it that he has the right and I don't.'

'He has the right to provide boarding schools and nannies…'

'That's what he's offering,' he said strongly. 'That's what I'm trying to prevent. Steven doesn't know him. Henry needs more than that.'

'So you're offering Peggy your home.'

'I am,' he said, strongly now. 'I believe a court could well come down on Peggy's side if she's settled over there. But, Meg, if Steven contests it, they might demand even more. An old lady… Me at weekends… It might not be enough.' He hesitated. 'Meg, if you come…there's more to my list of things that you might do.'

'Housekeeper?' she said astringently. 'I can't see that as a job description.'

'It wouldn't work,' he agreed. 'I can't see you changing careers to wash floors, and I already have a perfectly good housekeeper. And I've been thinking of problems. But there's another position going vacant.'

'You've said there are boat charter companies. Garden? Fish? What else could I do? And what problems?'

'There'll be visa restrictions,' he conceded. 'You might not be able to stay long term. But, if you were to come...if you were to see there could be a life there for you... I have this idea. It sounds crazy but I want you to think about it. It could be the solution to all our problems.'

'Which is?' To say she felt wary was an understatement. A huge understatement.

And she was right to be wary because his next statement floored her.

'Think this through,' he said, urgently now because maybe he could see by the expression on her face that she was already suspecting him of something dire. And here it came. 'Meg, I'm in the market for a wife and I think that wife could be you.'

CHAPTER TEN

IT WAS CLEARLY the most ridiculous thing she'd ever heard of.

She stared at him in astonishment, then rose and stared at him some more.

'Right,' she said at last, obviously deciding the whole proposition was ludicrous and acting accordingly. 'Did you take another of those travel sickness pills before the chopper ride? In rare cases they can cause hallucinations, so I'll give you the benefit of the doubt. I'll leave you to get over it. Goodnight, Matt.'

And she walked inside—or maybe bolted inside might be a better description. But then she closed the door carefully behind her, as if a sudden bang might unsettle a disordered mind even more.

Leaving him staring into the dark, unable to follow up with his very reasonable…reasoning.

What had he just said?

He didn't even know how the idea had come

to him. He'd been thinking through the visa options and marriage had just appeared. Like a light bulb being turned on.

Meg didn't seem to think it was a light bulb. To her it was nuts.

Maybe he shouldn't have sprung it on her quite so soon.

Yeah. He knew that was right, but the more he thought about it, the more it seemed…reasonable?

Marriage had always been there, in the back of his mind, as an option he'd get to sooner or later. Probably later. He'd met some amazing women but there'd never been a woman he wanted to wake up beside, morning after morning.

To share his life with.

To be honest, he wasn't thinking of sharing his life now. He never had. Solitude had been his way of life for so long he couldn't imagine himself changing.

But now he had a vision in his head that refused to go away.

The big house at the Hamptons was a house he'd always loved. As a kid it had seemed magic.

Once upon a time his grandparents had employed a gardener, Peter, a gentle guy with a limp and a smile and five kids. Matt's nanny had liked Peter and she'd liked Peter's kids, so Matt remembered a couple of school breaks where the house had come alive with adventure, noise, chaos.

Matt's mother had finally arrived midbreak and put an abrupt end to it, but Matt still remembered that feeling of...home.

He was thinking of it now. A house with Peggy and Henry and Stretchie and Boof.

And Meg.

A family to come home to.

He saw himself arriving from Manhattan and being swept up in family, dogs, laughter.

And Meg's smile.

Meg.

There was the siren call.

It was too soon. Far too soon to think about marriage. He'd known her for less than a week.

But part of him didn't think it was ludicrous. To part of him it was making complete sense.

He'd terrified her with his impulsive proposal. He needed to give her space now, but he was hopeful. Calm thought would surely show her what could be good for them all. Yes, a major proposition as marriage needed to be considered from every angle. But it was sensible. Wasn't it?

He rose and stared out into the night and the

more he thought about it, the more reasonable it seemed. Here, Meg had a lousy job and a load of debt. She'd admitted she was lonely. She'd opened her home to Peggy and Henry, and he could tell she was already opening her heart.

To him?

There was the rub. He didn't have a clue how she felt about him. But she'd admitted she also felt this…thing between them, this frisson of electricity that honestly he'd never felt before. Maybe it was because she was so far out of his orbit, almost another species from the glamorous women in his professional world. Or maybe it was the way she comforted Henry, she offered her home without a thought, the way Peggy instinctively trusted her.

Maybe it was the way Matt instinctively trusted her.

The way he wanted her.

And there was the bottom line, he thought, honesty surfacing. The idea of having a ready-made family at weekends was appealing. The idea of finding Meg in his bed was even more so.

'Yeah, back off,' he told himself. 'Let's put this as a proposition of sense, not of need.'

Need... There was an interesting word. It hovered uncertainly in his mind.

He didn't need anyone. He'd learned that a long time ago. So why did he hope...?

'Because of Henry,' he said out loud but Meg was there, front and foremost, and he knew he was a liar.

She lay in the dark in the bed she'd slept in for ever. She stared up at nothing in particular and she thought, *Matt just asked me to marry him.*

Just like that. Marriage.

She'd known him for how long? The man was clearly deluded.

Except he wasn't. The man was beautiful.

Was that a weird way to describe a guy? Maybe it was, but it was how she was starting to think of him. Physically he was gorgeous but that was only the start of it. The way he smiled at her... The way he held Henry... The way he cared... The way he'd held her back on the island...

The feel of his kiss...

Block that out, she told herself. Passion has nothing to do with sensible life decisions.

What he was suggesting was so far from sensible it was unthinkable.

Or was it?

Marriage to a guy she'd known for less than a week? How could that make sense?

But if it ended up being a feasible solution…

Suddenly she found herself drifting into the possibilities of maybe. What if?

This was fairy-tale stuff. A kid who left school at sixteen and caught fish for a living marrying a billionaire?

It was nonsense, but what if?

It'd be a Cinderella scenario, she told herself, and the story of Cinderella had always left her uneasy. What happened when the credits faded, the happy-ever-after disappeared from the screen and Cinders was left with an idle life in a world she wasn't born to?

But if she did let herself climb aboard that pumpkin coach… If she let herself be cared for by one Matt McLellan…

She didn't need to be cared for by anyone, she told herself. She was twenty-eight, independent, solid and…tough as old boots?

She was stuck in a lifestyle that was starting to feel more restrictive than an overtight corset. She was facing a life of either living in Rowan Bay while she paid down her debt or trying to make a living somewhere else. With what skills?

She thought of what she was doing now, taking parties of amateur fishermen out to sea, coping with seasickness, drunkenness, then crates of fish to be gutted because cleaning their fish was incorporated into the charter.

She didn't mind it too much. It was a living. But the thought of Peggy and Henry living with her had offered a sliver of how things might be. Of a life less lonely. That sliver had gone now, except Matt had offered an alternative.

A voice was suddenly whispering in the back of her mind. She could just see. She didn't have to commit. Cinders had fallen into her prince's arms and the deed had been done, but it didn't have to be like that. Could she go to the States, do Peggy's real estate inspection, just try?

She heard Matt's footsteps coming down the hall, heading to the bedroom she'd designated for him. And suddenly a decision was made. Without giving herself time to think, she was out of bed, opening the door. 'Matt?'

He was right by her door. Close. Large.

The passage footlight was on, shining upward. He was beautiful. He was right…there.

'Meg.' He sounded wary.

'It's an off-the-wall idea,' she said.

'It is,' he agreed. 'But it's just an idea.'

'We couldn't possibly agree to such a thing unless we got to know each other better.'

'I agree.'

It was a weird scenario. She was standing barefooted, clad in her flimsy nightgown. He was fully dressed in his new clothes, shaved now, contained, watchful.

Gorgeous.

She should back away.

She wasn't backing. This was the mature version of Cinderella, she told herself. She was twenty-eight and she was going for it.

'Matt?'

'Mmm?' He wasn't sure where to take this, she thought. He'd made the proposition and now… was he having second thoughts?

'You really are proposing marriage?'

'I'm saying we could think about it.'

'So I'm thinking.'

'That's good.'

'Matt…'

'Mmm?'

'You know when we stopped at the pharmacy for steroids for my cough?'

'I… Yes.'

'I didn't just buy steroids.'

'I see.' And suddenly the wariness was being edged out by laughter. 'You, too?'

'What do you mean, you, too?'

'Because while you were in the back waiting for your prescription to be filled, I was making my own purchase.'

'Oh.' She couldn't think what to say—or do—next.

'So now we seem to be equipped,' he said. 'Just in case.'

'I'm not agreeing to marriage. That'd be nuts.'

'It surely would. But getting to know each other better...' His hands came out and cupped her face. 'Meg, that'd be sensible.'

She didn't seem sensible. She seemed as if she were floating.

The feel of his hands... The warmth of his voice...

Oh, Cinders, she thought. *You might have been an idiot but I'm starting to figure you had no choice.*

'I won't pressure you,' Matt said, his voice serious again, and she found herself smiling.

'Suit yourself, Matt McLellan,' she told him. 'Because I believe I'm about to pressure you. You can't make a woman a proposition like that and then go calmly to bed.'

'I think I can,' he told her, and then, suddenly, his hands dropped from her face, his arms scooped under her, and she was lifted, held against him, and his laughter was all around them. Not out loud. Just there. Laughter and... love? 'I think I can,' he said again. 'It's just a matter of whose bed we go calmly to.'

'Forget the calm,' she managed. 'And your bed because it's bigger.'

It was a week before the results of Henry's DNA testing came through and it was a magic week.

Matt should be back in Manhattan. There was need for him to return but somehow the need to stay was greater.

It wasn't spoken pressure, though. For Matt it was the way Henry's eyes lit when he entered a room, the way Henry tentatively asked him if he could fish, the way he offered to show him what Meg had taught him.

It was the way Peggy deferred to him, depended on him, questioned him endlessly about what would happen. The way her voice wobbled as she bravely accepted her world had changed.

It was the way the two dogs bonded, tearing around the house like crazy things, annoying the chickens, bouncing as if the world was their constant delight.

But mostly it was the way Meg smiled at him. It was the way she folded into his body at night. The rightness of it.

The way her shabby, down-at-heel house felt like home.

Home seemed an insidious word, but more and more it centred around Meg. They didn't speak of marriage again—she backed away if he raised it and maybe she was right. No decision needed to be made yet. But suddenly Manhattan didn't seem as pressing. Staying with this makeshift family, being part of it, feeling as if he was making a difference in keeping Henry happy, in reassuring Peggy, in helping slash grass, collecting eggs, repairing a fence...

Lying with Meg. Feeling her curve against him. Being part of her.

Yes, it felt like home and when the results of the DNA came through—positive, as they'd all expected—he was even sorry.

But his plan meant this didn't end. It simply moved.

First things first—take Meg to McLellan Place. Show her how life could be.

Show her how a plan could become reality.

CHAPTER ELEVEN

IT WAS MEG'S first time in a plane and it left her stunned. Her bed, her seat, the service were all great. Her first-class pyjamas were pretty much the nicest pyjamas she'd ever worn and apparently she could keep them. She should be enjoying the whole experience.

She was lonely.

What had she expected? Maybe that they'd talk? Watch movies together? Just…share this fantastic experience.

Whatever, it wasn't happening. It was as if a switch had been flicked the moment Matt had stepped into the plane. 'Work's overwhelming,' he told her apologetically. 'I need to get a handle on what's happening before I land.'

A plane was obviously a place where he was accustomed to working. He surfaced for meals, he slept briefly, but for most of the time he used the plane's internet and 'got his handle'.

She peeked out of the windows—blinds were

pulled because they messed with the screens of Matt and the other seasoned travellers around her—and marvelled at the world beneath her.

And wondered more and more what she was getting herself into.

Marriage? The idea was seeming more and more like a pipe dream. Every time she looked, Matt seemed a world away, deep in his life of high finance.

He'd been dramatically pulled from work, she told herself as the long plane trip finally reached its end. Maybe she needed to cut him some slack.

'We'll go straight down to McLellan Place,' Matt told her as they landed. 'I'm needed in the city but Peggy will be eager to hear from you. McLellan Place is where I hope you can all live.'

'Where Peggy and Henry can live,' she retorted. 'There's no *me* in this equation yet.'

'I hope I can persuade you otherwise.'

'Matt—'

'Wait and see,' he said simply, so she shut up as they were streamlined through the airport, then as a chauffeured car drove them through the city, toward the increasingly beautiful country to his beachside home.

But once again Matt wasn't with her. For most

of the journey he was on the phone. 'Now I'm back I need to reschedule urgent meetings.'

'You're going to dump me and run?'

'I'll spend tonight and maybe tomorrow with you and then maybe you can come back to Manhattan with me. I have an apartment there. You'll get to see the whole package.'

She fell silent, doubts crowding in from all sides.

Peggy and Henry were back in Rowan Bay, fishing, exploring, making themselves at home, giving themselves time to get to know each other and come to terms with their shared grief. Maureen had promised to keep an eye on them, which would involve at least half a dozen visits a day. Boof remained with them, as did Stretchie. 'We're going to check out a for-ever home for you,' Matt had told Henry, and Meg knew Henry was beginning to feel safe enough to be left.

Meg, on the other hand, wasn't feeling the least bit safe. In fact she was feeling so unsafe that, when they finally pulled up before the magnificent gates of McLellan Place, it was as much as she could do not to bolt.

There was a house just inside the gates, but the car didn't even slow. 'That's the gatehouse,' Matt said, dismissively.

'Right,' she said faintly, looking at the house that was far bigger and grander than hers. 'For what, someone to live in while they open and shut the gates?'

'The gates work automatically now. Our head gardener lives there.'

Head gardener. Right.

She had no more questions.

The driveway seemed to stretch for ever, meandering through private woods, then opening to gardens that welcomed them in. And finally she saw the house, long, low, gracious...mellowed with age. She counted five gables, two together and then three, with a vast stretch of what looked like a pavilion in between. An enormous vine—wisteria?—ran the entire length of the gables, its drooping autumnal leaves accentuating the gold hue of magnificent stone steps.

It looked like something Meg had seen in magazines in doctors' waiting rooms. Not in real life.

'You don't really live here,' she breathed.

'Mostly I live in Manhattan.'

'Then who...?'

'It stays pretty much empty,' he told her. 'My great-grandparents used it for entertaining, as did my grandparents. My parents never liked the seclusion so they planned to sell but the seclusion suits me. I bought it from them ten years ago.'

'You bought it from your parents...' She was struggling to get her head around the dynamics of his family. Of this place. Of wealth beyond her comprehension.

'I was sent here most holidays,' he said. 'I've grown fond of it.'

'I could grow fond of the gatehouse,' she said frankly. 'To grow fond of this house...'

'You don't like it?'

'It's like a palace.' She turned to him, feeling totally confused. *Bewildered* wasn't a big enough word. 'Matt, why on earth would you want to marry me?'

There was silence at that. The car had pulled to a halt in the vast circular driveway. The driver opened the doors for them to alight and occupied himself taking their luggage into the house. Meg could see a woman—a housekeeper?—ushering him in.

What nonsense was this? With this amount of wealth, with these supports, Peggy and Henry would be safe for ever. They certainly didn't need her.

'Meg, it's just a house,' Matt said. 'If you came, you'd make it a home.'

Home.

She thought of home as she'd known it, before the accident, before loss and grief had robbed it of its heart. Her parents and grandparents had made her house a home.

She glanced back toward the vast gates that had seamlessly closed behind them. They were so far away she could no longer see them.

She shivered.

'Give it a chance,' Matt told her. 'Didn't your parents tell you not to judge on appearances?'

'Their vision of appearances didn't stretch to this,' she breathed. 'This is movie stuff.'

'This is home.'

'Here? By yourself?'

'I hope not,' he said seriously and took her face in his hands and kissed her. 'We could be happy here, Meg.'

'Could we?'

She was shown to her bedroom—sumptuous enough to make her gasp. The housekeeper who'd greeted them formally, but who'd disappeared almost the moment they'd arrived, had said lunch would be at twelve. Meg showered and changed into her best trousers and shirt and she still felt…not dirty, just small. Then she made her way cautiously back to the dining room. Taking in the house as she went.

The living rooms and bedrooms, the gleaming bathrooms, the windows leading out to the sea without a trace of salt on them, the acres of lawn and garden…there must be an army of 'housekeepers' keeping this place functioning.

To say she was unnerved was an understatement.

Matt was on the phone when she reached the dining room. He raised his brows in apology and waved to the table.

She sat and she felt smaller. This table was ridiculously big.

Matt finally finished his call.

'Is everything okay? Is your bedroom comfortable?' he asked.

Of all the questions to ask. She had eight—eight!—pillows to choose from. How could she not be comfortable?

She ate the most beautiful salmon salad she'd ever tasted in her life. There were tiny lemon meringues for desert. And grapes. And wine.

She very carefully didn't touch the wine.

'Jet lag,' she said when Matt offered to fill her glass and he raised his brows.

'You slept on the plane. Under a down duvet. With three pillows.'

'That was because I couldn't choose from the pillow menu. I can't choose here.' She stared at him in bewilderment. 'Matt, with all this, you could have any wife you wanted.'

'I want you.'

'How can you want me? I'm a nothing.'

'How can you say you're a nothing? You're everything I've ever wanted in a partner. Brave, beautiful, smart, funny, independent...'

'Is it the independent thing that makes me suitable?' she ventured. The loneliness thing was starting to get to her.

'I don't want a wife who clings, if that's what you mean.'

'I don't cling. But if I needed to cling...'

'I'd be there for you.' And his voice—and his expression—said he was serious.

'Don't do that.' She was starting to recover. The feistiness she seemed to have been born with—or the feistiness she'd developed almost as a shield as she'd struggled to survive by fishing in a mostly guys' world—was coming to her aid. 'Matt, there is this...thing between us but it's called lust. We've been thrown into each other's company in a weird way and it's messed with your judgement.'

'My judgement's never let me down in the past.'

'Well, it might have let you down now. Especially if you've judged that Peggy and Henry could be happy here. They'd… I don't know… wallow.'

'Wallow?'

'Lose each other. Echo. This place is vast.'

'It doesn't need to be vast. There's a guest wing at the end I thought they could use, two bedrooms with a sitting room between. It's cosy.'

'I don't know if I agree with your definition of *cosy.*'

'And there's the sea. If you've finished your meringues…'

'I might never finish these meringues,' she admitted. The one she was currently attending was a perfect crisp shell, cracking to reveal a marshmallow centre and at its heart a scoop of the most delicious lemon curd she'd ever tasted. There were still ten…twelve…on the plate. 'If I don't eat them will they be fed to the compost?'

'I have no idea,' he said faintly.

'Really?' She took another, almost defensively.

'I'll give orders that they're to be served at supper, as well.'

'You're kidding. You'll give orders...'

'I'll ask nicely. My staff are accommodating.'

'I bet they are.' She shook her head. 'Matt, this place is out of this world.'

'It's special,' he agreed. 'I need to show you the beach. Would you like a swim?'

'A swim.' She considered. She glanced out of the dining room window at the outside pool, then across to what looked like a vast pond, and, in the distance, the beach.

'The house pool is heated but the beach is better. I know it's autumn but the water shouldn't be too cold. Not after the water you're used to.'

She finished her meringue and tried very hard not to be seduced by the zing of lemon, by the soft marshmallow, by the crisp outer shell... By the smile of the man watching her from the other side of the table. Who'd spent almost all of the last twenty-four hours on his laptop or on his phone.

'Will you come with me?'

'Yes.'

'Will you bring your phone?'

He glanced at his phone, lying on the table beside him, and then he looked at her. Decision time?

'I won't,' he said. Supreme sacrifice? 'We can walk to the beach or we can take the boat.'

'I'd like to walk,' she told him.

They walked around the cultivated shore path that bordered the pond and led to the sea. The path was a thing of beauty on its own, Meg thought, with coastal grasses, trees seemingly sculpted by the winds, vast rocks scattered as if the sea had thrown them there. It was only her knowledge of true wild seascapes that told her this was landscaping brilliance.

She'd donned her bathing gear under her jeans and T-shirt. She was a guest of Matt and she was heading for a swim. There was no reason why her knees were shaking.

It's jet lag, she told herself, but she knew it was no such thing.

'It's gorgeous,' she managed. She'd been walking for ten minutes with Matt striding silently beside her and she needed to say something. Anything.

'It is.' And she could hear the pride in his voice.

'That one man could own this... And hardly share...'

'I am offering to share,' he told her. 'That's why you're here.'

She shut up again.

And then they reached the beach and her world seemed to settle.

It was always like this. As a child she remembered getting home from school and racing down to the beach. Sometimes she'd swim or walk one of the legion of O'Hara dogs. But often she'd just sit, doodling in the sand, savouring the feel of the sun on her face...or simply being. The wash of the waves, the immensity of the ocean, the timelessness, soothed something inside her so deep, so intrinsic that she knew she could never leave the ocean.

That was why she couldn't sell her grandparents' house and walk away from her debts. Where else could she be by the ocean every day of her life? In the city, maybe, or a decent-sized tourist town? Sure, she could rent herself a bedsit, make herself a life. She could walk on the beach with other tourists.

It was totally selfish, this feeling that the ocean was hers.

'You love it, don't you?' Matt asked gently, and she could only nod.

She expected him to continue. She expected more pressure. Instead he said simply, 'Swim?'

And he kicked off his shoes, tugged off his shirt and trousers and headed for the sea.

She stayed for a moment, watching. He walked straight in and then dived. The waves here were small, the cove protected by two headlands. There was no sign of anyone, of anything. A private beach? She'd heard of such places.

Did he own all this?

He'd disappeared, sleek, smooth, sliding underwater, only the faintest break in the surface occurring when he needed to breathe.

She could see seagrasses from here. A sheltered rocky cove… It'd be home for so much.

What was she doing, standing gawping at a guy like Matt when she could be checking out seagrasses?

She gave herself a mental shake—which kind of didn't work because she was still thinking of Matt, of his gorgeous body, of the way he'd slid into that wave as if he'd been born to the sea…

But she had to ignore it. There was a whole new ocean world to explore.

And Matt McLellan was surely only an incidental part.

He had his life sorted. She just had to see it.

From the moment the idea had come into his head, there'd been not a single doubt that this was the right decision. Matt McLellan was known for decisiveness. It had never let him down in the past and it wasn't letting him down now. The path he saw in front of him was perfect.

He'd grown fond—okay, very fond—of the little boy who'd sat in his office, who'd spent so much time with him. The thought of Henry being an 'extra child' to a father who'd sounded responsible on the phone but not emotionally involved left him cold. Henry needed a family.

More than that, Peggy needed a home, and in the days since he'd met her he'd grown to like her. She loved her little grandson.

But Henry needed more. He needed a Meg. A woman who cared, who'd take over the reins as Peggy grew older. The three of them would love McLellan Place. It'd come to life again.

And Meg would be here.

That was the part of the equation that wasn't so straightforward. For her to stay seemed a viable solution to her problems and to his need to have someone here for Peggy and Henry. And yet it was much more than that.

He had to give her space. In business deals he knew when too much pressure threatened a deal and he could sense it now.

But hell, he wanted to pressure. Because this was perfect.

Meg was perfect?

A fisherwoman from Australia, wife to the heir to the McLellan fortune? His mother would have forty fits.

But at a deeper level his mother wouldn't care. Since when had she ever cared?

Meg would care. That was the thing. From the moment he'd met her, he'd known that caring was Meg's special skill. Her warmth, her humour, her passion… The generosity of her lovemaking. The way she held him…

That was the thing that had somehow slipped under his skin, into his heart? She smiled at him and he thought she didn't give a toss about who he was, how much he owned, what his family represented. She was simply Meg, holding Matt.

A huge part of him was telling him to march

back up the beach right now, sweep her into his arms and carry her back to the house. Hold her. Claim her.

What was he, a Neanderthal? But that was how she made him feel, and when he saw her slip into the water to be with him, the urge was so great it took every ounce of his self-control to keep swimming.

The seagrasses here had held him fascinated for years and they should hold him fascinated now. They changed every time he visited. His attention should be on them because turning and taking Meg into his arms was *not* on the agenda.

Luckily, once he motioned to the grasses, she turned her attention downward.

She swam as well as he did—maybe better. Snorkels and masks would be good. He should have brought them with him, but yeah, he'd been distracted. Luckily Meg didn't seem to need them. She was using her arms to sweep forward underwater. Her copper curls wisped around her face. Her body, lithe, slim, beautiful in a simple black bathing costume, was entrancing.

And then she saw the turtles. Her arms stilled. She floated forward and he thought, *She has to breathe sometime...*

Usually the turtles held him entranced. These

were little more than hatchlings, floating over and through the rafts of seagrasses, feeding on the tiny sea creatures or on the grass itself.

He'd seen them first when he was about the same age as Henry. They were almost unheard of at this latitude, but the protection of the bay and the warmth of the currents seemed to provide a haven where they flourished. They'd always held him entranced.

As they held Meg entranced. She floated, breathing only when she had to.

He remembered the last woman he'd brought here. Lauren was a high-flying lawyer, whip-smart, with an acerbic wit he found incredibly sexy. She was also beautiful. They'd dated for six months and he'd fleetingly thought maybe they could take things further.

But then he'd brought her here for a week's break.

He'd brought her to this beach and shown her the hatchlings. *How sweet*, she'd said, but she'd headed back to the beach almost straight away. *I'm not wasting tanning time on turtles, sweet as they are.*

Back at the house she'd explored the empty rooms and said, *Why don't we invite...?*

In comparison, Meg looked as if she could float

for hours. It had to be Matt who finally broke the moment. He had business calls to make—of course. Promise or not, business called.

'I need to get back to the house,' he said as they trod water and Meg smiled happily at him.

'That's okay. You go back. I'll come when I'm ready.'

That was another eye-opener. What woman had ever said something like that to him?

She was independent. He liked that.

He needed that.

'But tell me about the turtles first,' she begged. 'Are they Kemp's ridley?' Had she recognised the distinctive heart-shaped shell?

'They are.'

'These are practically hatchlings. Is this a nesting site? I thought the only nesting sites were in Mexico.'

She really did know her turtles!

'And here,' he said.

'I've never heard of them nesting anywhere else.'

'Nobody has,' he told her. 'That's a huge reason why I can't sell this place. Once out of my hands, who knows what will become of it? These are incredibly endangered. The environmental authorities know they nest here, but no one else. This place is an environmental haven and I'll protect it with every means at my disposal. That's the biggest reason I bought it when my parents wanted to sell.'

'So you don't really need a mansion?' she said, treading water, watching his face. 'You want a turtle nursery.'

'I don't want it turned into a resort, if that's what you mean. This place is special.'

And then he paused and thought, Why not say it?

'Meg… If you agree to come here… If you agree to marry me, then you'll be taking on that responsibility, too. You'll be guardian to the piping plovers, who also nest in the dunes, and to the turtle hatchlings. If I can't persuade you to marry me because of Henry and Peggy, how about plovers and turtles?'

It was a joke. Sort of. He expected her to smile. Instead she gave him a look that was puzzled. Questioning. He wasn't sure what the question was but she didn't take it further.

'Leave it, Matt,' she said simply. 'Go make those business calls and let me play with turtles.'

And before he could say anything else she duck-dived downward. She was back underwater and he was left to make his way home alone.

* * *

In the end she had a fabulous day, floating, swimming, sleeping on the sand. Eating on the terrace under the stars. Talking to Matt about the things she discovered he cared about—amazingly he left his phone inside. Abandoning her bedroom because who needed two?

They slept that night in the most luxurious bed she could imagine. She slept in the arms of a man she was starting to believe she loved.

His body was everything she'd ever dreamed of. His voice, his touch, his tenderness, his passion... It must be a dream, she told herself as they loved until exhaustion finally had them drifting to contented, sated sleep.

Yes, she'd been lonely, but if she could have him like this... She abandoned herself to the belief that maybe the dream could become reality.

But reality had a way of poking its nose in. In the small hours she woke and headed to the bathroom. His en suite bathroom was bigger than her Rowan Bay living room. The bath looked like a claw-footed, gleaming white island, surrounded by a sea of white marble. The shower could accommodate a small family. It was all glass and chrome. There were two enormous vanity basins. And walls of mirrors.

She headed back to bed shivering, and as she did she saw Matt's phone blinking on his bedside table. She'd figured it by now. Blinking meant work.

'Everyone has work,' she told herself as she headed across the white pile carpet and dived back into bed. 'And this is just a house, even if it is over the top.'

Matt stirred and reached out for her. His arms enfolded her and she felt herself drift back into the dreaminess of being held by such a man.

But it was a dream. The crazy bathroom was out there, reality, luxury she could scarcely imagine.

The phone was on the bedside table.

'It'll be okay if Matt's beside me,' she told herself as she drifted back to sleep. 'If Matt holds me...'

It would work, Matt thought as he lay in the dark and held the woman he'd hardly imagined could exist. This was his perfect woman. His perfect wife?

With Henry here, and Peggy and the dogs, maybe with children of their own, this place could come to life. It could be a living, laughing home. He'd come down at weekends and it'd welcome him. Meg would welcome him.

She could come to Manhattan if she wanted, he thought, but he wasn't sure how she'd fit there. The social side of his financial world wasn't particularly welcoming, and she'd be a fish out of water, but if she wanted…

He'd talk to her. In the morning.

Morning. He'd intended to head back to the city but he had the wisdom to realise he couldn't leave yet.

He'd sensed her unease. She was uncomfortable right now, stunned by the immensity of the place, its opulence, its sheer difference from the world she was used to. He'd be a fool if he hadn't figured it, and he'd be a fool if he messed things up now for want of trying.

What to do about it?

His phone lay on the bedside table, a tiny light winking, telling him that even though he'd worked today, messages were building up.

But Meg… The future…

He needed to stay for a couple more days, he decided. For now Meg needed to be his priority.

And wasn't that what he wanted? Just to hold her.

To hold on to the dream.

CHAPTER TWELVE

MATT HADN'T BEEN able to spare the days he'd spent taking Henry to Peggy, or the days he'd spent at Meg's. He rang Helen first thing and heard her astonishment.

'Two more days?'

'Three at the most,' he said placatingly. 'Then I'm back full-time.' His absence was causing huge problems but he needed Meg to decide this was a good place to live.

Not because of Henry, though. Meg was already agreeing that Peggy and Henry could be happy here. Her job as Peggy's envoy was done.

'Though they might be happier living somewhere like the gatehouse,' she ventured. 'This place echoes.'

'This place needs you,' he told her, but she looked doubtful.

But in typical Meg style, she set about enjoying herself. She swam with the turtles. She kayaked and she walked the beach. He had the groundsmen find fishing tackle so she could try her hand at fishing. He was with her as often as he could manage, but when he couldn't he had one of the gardeners make sure she wasn't alone. He saw her out of the windows making friends with them.

He watched her doing her best to feel at home.

The weather changed and the nights turned autumnal. Night dining on the terrace was no longer an option and Meg decreed she loathed the dining room.

She suggested they eat in what his grandfather used to call the snug. The room had been his grandfather's retreat when his grandmother's socialising went over the top. It had faded sofas, favourite paintings, an open fire, an oversized television. They ate and he tried to make time to watch old movies with her. They talked. Sometimes they made it to bed and made love and sometimes they didn't make it that far.

She didn't complain, though, when he left her to make his calls, to work in his study.

She wasn't needy.

After three days he was feeling more and more that this was working. He was starting to feel as if he'd found a woman who could be part of his life for ever.

Problem sorted? Time to move on? His life needed to resume and the demands from Manhattan could no longer be ignored.

Meg's plan was that she'd stay for two weeks. At least, that had been her plan on coming here. *His* plan was that she'd stay for ever, but he had the sense not to push.

Thinking ahead, she'd need time to pack up her belongings at Rowan Bay. Maybe in a few weeks he could snatch a little more time off and go back to Australia with her. He could put Peggy and Henry onto a cruise liner and then bring Meg home for ever.

Home. For ever. The words felt good. No, they felt great. McLellan Place had never seemed so alive as it did now that Meg was here. But work was imperative. Besides, he needed to be honest about how their life long term would be.

'I do need to head back to Manhattan,' he told her. 'I can come back at the weekend. Would you like to come with me or will you stay here?'

The weather had turned warm again and they'd been lying on the beach, sharing a beach rug. There might just have been a little lovemaking involved. He'd had one of the gardeners set up a sunshade, which was just as well.

'Because there are places I have no intention

of getting sunburned,' she'd retorted as she'd sunk into his arms. They'd fallen asleep after laughter and woken to bliss.

Now, though, the words had to be said. The real world was breaking in.

'Back to Manhattan,' she said sleepily, but he heard a note of caution in her voice.

'It's where I work.'

'That's surely too far to commute, nine to five.'

'My work's not nine to five.'

'So you actually live in Manhattan.'

'This is my home.'

'You're here at weekends.'

'Most weekends.' Some.

'And if Peggy and Henry come here…'

'Peggy's independent. Henry can go to the local school. I can put in place as many supports as they need.'

'And you say you want me, too.'

'I do.' And then he thought, Why wait for the champagne and roses, the perfect moment? He'd already raised it. Why not say it formally? 'Meg, you do know I'd like to marry you. It seemed sensible back in Australia. It seems even more sensible now. So… Meg O'Hara, will you marry me?'

What followed was a troubled silence. This wasn't going well, he thought, and he had the sense to realise it.

She sat up and tugged her T-shirt on, almost as if she needed to be dressed to say what had to be said.

'I told you that my boss's son asked me to marry him just before all this happened,' she said, almost casually.

'He's obviously a man of taste.' He wasn't sure where she was going. 'I can't fault him on reasoning.'

'Yeah, that's it.' Her gaze met his head-on, but her eyes seemed troubled. 'I told you his reasons. They were sensible. Just like yours, only different.'

'I'd like to think that difference is huge.'

'Yeah, I get a bigger house and I don't have to gut Graham's fish.' She shook her head. 'No, that's not fair. The truth is, Matt, that I've fallen for you. Hard. I think… I think… I could even love you.'

Love. That was a word to take his breath away.

Did he even know what it meant? He still wasn't sure but now wasn't the time to say it.

'Then what…?' he ventured.

'Because I want the fairy tale.' The words

came out too fast, too loud, and she bit her lip, seeming to almost cringe as she heard them. 'No. That's not true. It's no fairy tale. My gran and grandpa had it and so did Mum and Dad. There were no mansions, no double washbasin made of marble, no walk-in his-and-hers dressing rooms, no acres of gardens and staff to match. But they used to hug. All the time. When Dad walked into the room, Mum's eyes used to light up. She'd just drop everything and hug.'

'Your dad was a fisherman, right?' he asked cautiously. 'I'd imagine he spent days at sea.'

'He did,' she conceded. 'And so did Grandpa. When they could, Mum and Grandma would go, too, but sometimes they couldn't. And that's what I've been thinking. I'm figuring that what you're proposing is like the old days, for me to be here keeping the candle burning for your return.'

It was. 'Is that selfish? You could have a great life here, Meg. A far easier life than the one you have in Rowan Bay.'

'I know that,' she said uneasily. 'Matt, these few days…they've been wonderful but I'm still… There are still things I need to know.' She closed her eyes for a moment and then she opened them, decision made. She pushed herself to her feet.

'Okay,' she conceded. 'When Dad was at sea Mum always knew exactly where he was, what he was doing. Take me to Manhattan and show me the other side of your life.'

The chopper took them back to Manhattan early the next morning. He'd normally head straight to the office, but he took Meg to his apartment first.

Which didn't go as well as he'd have liked.

Matt thought of the night he'd brought Henry back here. There'd been a choice then: hand Henry over to Social Services or take him home himself. He'd walked into his apartment with the bewildered, shocked Henry and he'd wished the place had seemed more homey. Now, as he ushered Meg through the ornate foyer into his elegant sitting room, he wished the same.

'It's just a place to crash,' he told her and wondered why he sounded apologetic. 'I need to get a decorator in, make it seem a bit more kid-friendly.'

'Can a decorator do that?' Meg crossed to the picture windows opening to vistas of New York.

'How? Replace your Pre-Raphaelite paintings with Pooh Bear and Eeyore?'

Pre-Raphaelite?

His grandfather had started Matt's art collection and Matt had added to it. Local dealers gave him a heads-up when good pieces came up for auction. They were a good investment. Impressive. Solid.

'Do you like them?' he asked cautiously, aware of his prejudiced surprise that she even knew the label.

'Nope.' She finished checking the paintings in the living room, glanced into the dining room to see more, and she shuddered.

'Or yes,' she conceded. 'They're brilliant, of course. But, Matt, they should be in a museum somewhere, not oppressing the bejeezers out of everyone who walks in here.'

Oppressing? He'd thought impressing more like.

'I'm sorry you disapprove.' He heard himself stiffening, ancestral pride doing a double take.

'I disapprove of so much money being tied up for one man to look at over his morning toast.'

'I eat my toast in the kitchen.'

'Bully for you. Are there Pre-Raphaelites there, too?'

'Dada,' he said, and she shot him a look of incredulity and headed through to see. Satirical, nonsensical, the Dada paintings were part of a collection he'd begun himself.

'Oh, my.' Meg stopped before a picture of a pair of eyes somehow superimposed on a twisted teapot. 'This is just the thing to face after a hard night.'

'Maybe not,' he conceded. 'But I eat my breakfast fast.'

'I would, too, just to get out of here.'

'I'll replace it before Henry comes here,' he said defensively, and she turned and gave him a long, hard look.

'Do you like this stuff?'

'It's an excellent investment. I can't see Pooh and Eeyore fitting in here.'

'I can't see anyone but you fitting in here.'

'As I said, I'll get a designer in.'

'It doesn't need a designer,' she said bluntly. 'It needs someone to treat it as home. Look at that refrigerator. Have you ever seen a fridge as big as that without at least one grubby note attached saying there's a Save the Whale meeting at your neighbours' next Thursday? Or a change to garbage schedule? Or a card for a friend who's turned clairvoyant and you promised you'd spread the word to your other friends who drop in unannounced with a slab of beer to watch a footy game?' She looked at him a moment longer and then shook her head.

'Uh-oh. Matt, you don't have a clue about your neighbours, do you?'

'I… No.' He was at the apartment so little, and his entrance was private.

'And mates who watch footy here? No?' She sighed. 'Okay, bring in your designer but keep an open mind about the fridge. Maybe let Henry decorate it. Meanwhile, are you heading to the office?'

'I am,' he conceded, but the thought of leaving Meg by herself with the Dadas… He hadn't thought this through. 'What will you do?'

'Not sit here and let a teapot stare at me, that's for sure. I'll go explore.'

'I'll put the car at your disposal.'

'No, thanks.' She said it fast. 'Shanks' pony is great for seeing. So you'll be back for dinner?'

This wasn't the way to encourage thoughts of marriage, he conceded. He should have left her at McLellan Place.

'I'm meeting Steven Walker for lunch,' he told her and watched her expression change.

'Henry's father? Really?'

'Yeah.' He'd had a few calls with Steven. Things were slotting into place, but a formal meeting seemed appropriate.

'Would you like me to come with you?'

'I don't know.' He hesitated. 'Meg, until... Unless you commit to helping care for Henry, it might give the wrong impression. We don't want to come across as a ready-made family.'

'We certainly don't.' She eyed him cautiously.

'But if you'd like to meet Steven...'

'I would.'

'Then I'll send the car for you at one.'

'Tell me the address and I'll get there myself.' He saw her glance down at the clothes she was wearing—neat jeans and a white shirt. 'That settles what I'll do this morning. I obviously need some going-to-lunch-with-billionaires clothes.'

'Steven's not a billionaire.'

'You've looked him up, too? Okay, multimillionaire. Practically on the breadline. Regardless I'm not going to lunch looking like the poor relation.'

'Try Neiman Marcus,' he suggested. 'Or Bloomingdale's. I have accounts there. I'll give you my card.'

'You're kidding me, right? Is this a *Pretty Woman* moment?'

'I can afford—'

'I'm sure you can but so can I.' She grinned and stepped forward and kissed him, a proprietorial kiss, short and sweet and far too fast. When she stepped back she was still smiling.

'Believe it or not, I can dress myself,' she told him. 'Allow me some dignity. Do you have somewhere here I can check the internet? Of course you do. The security code I saw you punch in—is that all I need to get in and out of this apartment? Great. Okay, off you go and cope with the world's financial convolutions while I go find something to wear. I know what I think is more fun.'

Steven Walker was pretty much as Matt had expected. He was in his fifties, well built but bordering on pudgy. His Italian suit looked as if it had been made for him, his aura was one of wealth and privilege, and he spoke with care, as if whatever was said could be used against him. He greeted Matt as a business associate, and Matt could see the reservations behind the man's eyes.

That was okay. Matt had reservations, too. This was uncharted territory. Negotiating the fate of one small boy...

He'd chosen one of his favourite eateries, discreet, expensive, a restaurant with myriad 'rooms' where business could be talked without fear of being heard. Maybe that had been a mistake, though, he thought, as the waiter hovered and asked about the absent 'third person'. This wasn't business. Or was it?

Whatever, by the time they were through their first beer he was conscious of escalating tension. They'd been edging around the topic of Henry. Neither of them knew where to take this. To Matt it seemed as if they were marking time. Waiting?

And then Meg arrived and the sight of her seemed to settle something deep within. It was all he could do to keep it formal, not to step forward and take her into his arms.

She looked amazing.

He'd expected her to be wearing, what? Something vaguely corporate? Not so much. She'd headed out with the idea of shopping for a business-type lunch in Manhattan. What she'd come up with was pure Meg.

When he'd first seen her she'd been in filthy jeans, a battered oilskin and bare feet. What she was wearing now wasn't even close to what she'd been wearing then, nor to the shabby jeans and windcheaters she'd worn back at Rowan Bay, but she'd lost nothing of that original, indomitable Meg.

She was wearing black tights with ankle-length boots made of soft charcoal leather. Her crimson skirt was short, crisp, neat, showing off her gorgeous legs. A black vest lay beneath a beautiful embroidered jacket. The jacket was a little shorter than her vest, making the outfit look eye-catchingly chic. A faded leather bag—he recognised the brand and did a double take—hung casually from her arm.

To top it off, she'd obviously found time to have her copper curls shaped into a proper elfin trim.

She looked happy, buzzy from a successful shop? Her eyes were glowing. She smiled brightly at him, and as both men rose she turned that glowing smile onto Steven.

'You're Steven? Henry's dad? I'm so pleased to meet you.'

Steven put out a pudgy paw; he held Meg's hand a little too long, and it was as much as Matt could do not to swipe it away and say, 'She's mine.'

He didn't. They were much too civilised. They sat again, and Matt tried not to look at Meg while she beamed at the waiter and asked nicely for a soda water, while she made small talk with Steven—while she held him entranced.

Gorgeous didn't begin to cut it.

'We need to talk about Henry,' he managed as their food arrived—the restaurant's speciality, a seafood platter to be shared.

'Let's.' Meg selected a scallop with care and popped it into her mouth. 'Yum. Tell us, Steven, are you upset about what's happening? And how do you see the care of your son playing out?'

They were good questions. Great questions. They left Steven no choice but to put his cards on the table.

'It's been a shock,' Steven admitted. He was watching Meg select an oyster and once again Matt had that almost-primeval urge to slap him. 'I'll admit my first emotion was anger that Amanda didn't tell me. But there's nothing I can do about that now, and I'll do what's right by the boy. He's my son and I want him under my eye. I've been trying to decide what's right, and I believe I have it sorted.'

'Tell us,' Meg said, seemingly entranced, and Steven flushed with the warmth of her attention.

'I'm a wealthy man,' he told her. 'And what's happened isn't the boy's fault. He is my son.

I've therefore decided that it's only fair that he'll inherit. I have six children already, from three wives, but I'm fair. My estate was to be split six ways. It'll now be split seven.'

'That's generous,' Meg told him with a sideways glance at Matt. 'But that's for when you're dead. What about now?'

'My current wife has enough on her hands with her...*our* two children,' Steven said smoothly, as if this was something that he'd worked out with care. 'And, of course, my children from previous marriages still have a call on me. My time's limited to attend to this boy's needs. As long as his grandmother moves here, I see no reason why he shouldn't stay with her. I've checked out McLellan Place on the web and he's a lucky child to be invited to live there. I'll pay for schooling, of course. He can go to the school I attended. It teaches boys to be boys—he can't do better.'

'Really,' Meg murmured. 'Boys will be boys, eh?'

'None of that "caring sharing" stuff,' Steven said, expanding on his theme. 'My son should be tough. Boarding school, of course. Not that you'd want him all the time. Boarding school's great until they turn into real human beings.'

Matt's hand slipped on his glass. He was gripping too hard. He carefully put it down. Smashing a glass would help nothing.

But Steven wasn't noticing tension. 'I'll cover any other costs he incurs, of course,' he said genially. 'After-school care, summer camps, that sort of thing. Oh, and of course, I'd like to meet him. Could his grandmother bring him into town, maybe once a month? Lunch? An hour or so? Kids aren't much company but you do need to make an effort.'

'You do,' Matt said. Tightly.

'So that's agreed?' The man seemed to relax, ground rules sorted. 'I can't help thinking Amanda used me, but I'll do what's right.'

'What's right,' Meg said thoughtfully and turned to Matt. 'An hour a month and funding. And no caring and sharing. Okay, Matt, your turn. What do you think's right for Henry?'

The seafood platter was excellent. The calamari was a little tougher than she liked, but then this place wouldn't be able to catch a squid a couple of hours before lunch.

She ate two calamari rings and another oyster while she waited for Matt's response. She knew this man by now. She could see tension in the set of his shoulders as he thought through Steven's…offer?

It was a crap offer but did he have a choice but to accept? Steven had the upper hand—there was nowhere for Matt to go.

This seemed like negotiating a business contract, Meg thought suddenly, and she didn't like the analogy.

Neither did Matt. She could see the tension on his face. She could see him thinking how to respond.

'Steven, what you're suggesting seems adequate,' he said at last. He was speaking slowly, and she could see him thinking each word out before he spoke. 'This way he'll have three adults in his life, his father, his grandmother, and me. I admit, I'd still like to be involved. You know Amanda was on my staff? Henry's been in and out of my office since he was a toddler. I've grown fond of him.'

'I understand that,' Steven said. 'If he's a son of mine he'll be whip-smart. If I get him well educated he'll be a son to be proud of.'

'I think that, too,' Matt said smoothly. 'But then…you already have children and you're a busy man. You'd have trouble fitting him into your schedule.'

'I'll make the time,' Steven said. 'My wife won't like it but it's a duty.'

'Does it have to be?' Matt said, tentatively now. 'You're doing what's right, but there is an alternative. It's possibly too soon to commit to such a thing but if the placement I'm proposing works out... If you and your wife agree... There may be another way forward. You have six children and I have none. Steven, once you've checked us out thoroughly, and I know you'd want to do that, how would you feel about allowing us to adopt him?'

What?

Meg sat back in her chair and let the words sink in. Or tried to.

Adoption?

Where had that come from?

And he'd just said...*us*?

And it seemed Steven was as astounded as she was. 'You're kidding?' He stared at Matt as if he'd just said something crazy. 'You realise if you adopted him you'd be responsible? School fees, the lot. More, he'd end up with a claim on the McLellan estate.'

Here we go, Meg thought numbly. Money.

'I'm happy for that to happen,' Matt said smoothly. He'd put his proposition on the table.

Now he sounded ready to negotiate the finer points. 'But the most important thing is surety for the boy. Peggy's elderly and edging on confused. Hopefully she'll be here for him for a few years yet, but, if not, this would give Henry the sense of belonging I think he needs.' He glanced across at Steven. 'Of course, you'd still like access, and it's important for Henry to know as much about his background as possible. A scheduled meeting with him once a month would still be an option.'

'Of course,' Steven said, and Meg watched him visibly warm to the idea. Ridding himself of a responsibility he'd never wanted in the first place. 'So he'd stay with you?'

'He'd stay at McLellan Place with Meg. I'd be there as much as I can.'

'With Meg?' He turned to Meg, bemused. 'This young lady? Where do you fit in?'

'Meg's Australian,' Matt said smoothly. 'Peggy's sent her as envoy to see for herself what we've arranged.' He hesitated but then obviously decided to say it. 'I'm trying to persuade Meg to move to McLellan Place, as well. As my wife.'

And just like that, Meg's shock turned to anger. What was he doing, saying such things to a guy she'd only just met? This was personal.

Plus…adoption. He hadn't even mentioned the option to her. He was talking of marriage and a child, and he hadn't even thought to talk about something so important?

'So there'd be a mom for Henry,' Steven said, his eyes alight with interest. 'Marriage, eh? The fast research I've done puts you as a confirmed bachelor. What's made you change your mind?'

'Meg has,' Matt said simply. 'With Meg at McLellan House, Henry would definitely be lucky.'

Lucky? Define *lucky*, Meg thought, thinking of that vast mansion, of the empty rooms, of Matt's apartment here, of the sterility, of the loneliness…

And then she thought, *Who am I thinking of as being lonely? Henry? Or Matt?*

Or me?

She was struggling to get her head around this. He'd proposed marriage. He'd create a family, for him to be part of at will?

'But you'd only be there at weekends,' she managed. She was blocking Steven out for the moment, focusing on the man in front of her. Marriage? Adoption? What was he promising Steven?

She was being blackmailed.

'My life is here in Manhattan, but yes, I'd be there whenever I can find time,' Matt told her.

And she thought, *He doesn't get it. He doesn't see.*

'Your life's in Manhattan?' She was having trouble getting her voice to produce more than a squeak.

'I have a business empire to run,' Matt said smoothly. He sounded back in control again, contract laid out; all she had to do was sign. 'I'll take care of Henry as well as I'm able but my financial empire is based here. That's who I am.'

'Bullshit.'

She said it far too loudly. The waiter, who'd surreptitiously arrived to check on drinks, stopped dead in the doorway. He checked the contents of their glasses from afar and disappeared fast.

This restaurant was obviously geared to respectful discretion. It probably wasn't used to having Australian fishing persons swearing at two financial giants.

These men were at the peak of their careers, she thought bleakly. They were powerful and ready to have every suggestion applauded by minions. So here she was, being blackmailed into being...a wife minion.

He hadn't talked to her about the adoption option. Why?

Because he'd decided to slot her into what he needed from her. Sharing? Not so much.

Enough. She wasn't tasting this seafood anyway. She rose and the men rose with her. Matt even had the decency to look worried. 'Is everything okay?'

'It's not okay,' she told him. She was trying not to let her voice wobble but she wasn't succeeding. 'Steven, I'd appreciate it if you could forget what Matt said about marriage. It's not going to happen. I came here to check that Henry would be cared for if he moved here and I know that'll happen. You guys sort the financials. Peggy will do the loving. And me? I'm heading back to my old life. Heaving craypots. Taking punters on fishing charters. I'd like to say that's who I am, but it's not true. It's what I do.'

'What are you saying?' Matt was looking at her in bewilderment. 'Meg, you could have a great life at McLellan Place.'

'I could, couldn't I?' she retorted. What she had to say shouldn't be said in front of Steven but what the heck? She was too angry to care.

'But where's what I *am* in that equation?' she demanded. 'Matt, crayfishing, fishing charters, they're what I do. They're not who I am. I'm a woman who was truly loved by my parents and by my grandparents. I'm a woman who's increasingly falling for one little boy. I'm also a woman who's watched Peggy agree to change her whole life because of love. That's what you're asking of me, too, Matt, and yes, I could do that. But here's the thing. McLellan Place, Henry, Peggy, me... We'd fit in around the edges of who you think you are. You call the shots and we jump to.'

'Meg—'

'Don't stop me.' Rejecting a man's marriage proposal in front of strangers was not the kindest thing to do, but then, had it been a marriage proposal? This was a business lunch. Matt was the one who'd linked marriage with adoption in front of Steven. He'd made it into a contract. It felt as if he was blackmailing her into agreeing—and it wasn't going to happen.

'Matt, you asked me to marry you and that's quite a coup for a woman like me,' she told him. 'But I'd be the wife who fitted around the edges of who you are and that's not what I want. I've seen my parents' marriage, and my grandparents'. They truly loved, and work had to fit around that. If I married you I'd be fitting around the edges of what really matters to you. And if you adopt Henry I'd see him fitting around your life in exactly the same way.'

'Meg!' Matt looked appalled, as well he might. Steven was practically goggling.

'It's okay,' she said, anger being superseded by a weariness that seemed bone deep. 'I understand, Matt, I truly do. You've made a great offer. I know you'll do what you're capable of for Henry, because you're an honourable man. But me... I want the fairy tale. I'll admit, I'm close to being head over heels in love with you and that feeling's only going to get deeper. But love doesn't work the way you see it. It's not something that's there for the weekends. It's for ever.'

'Meg, this is not the place. Could we talk about this later?'

'You've made it the place and there's not going to be a later,' she told him. She turned to Steven. 'It was good to meet you,' she said. 'You and Matt seem to have Henry's life sorted. I'll head back to Australia and tell Peggy that life at McLellan Place could be awesome. And it could be awesome, Matt, but it's not for me. If I said yes now, I'd be hauled even deeper into caring for Henry. Most of all, Matt McLellan, I've be hauled into loving you. I'd be hauled into needing to share your life. My parents had it. My grandparents had it and I'm willing to leave because I want it, too. I think I love you already, Matt McLellan, but I won't be a part-time wife.'

'That's not what I'm suggesting,' Matt said explosively.

'So what are you suggesting? Having a family… How do you see that changing your life?'

'It wouldn't need to. At least…'

'Least? Yep, you'd do the least possible to keep us all happy. We wouldn't be part of who you are.' She glanced at the still-goggling Steven and what she had to say firmed. 'Matt, I bet Steven married like that, and he's on his third wife. So here's the thing,' she said, desolation sweeping in to squash out the myriad emotions she was already dealing with. 'Love should change. It's changing me and it scares me. If I were to be your part-time wife I might just end up breaking my heart.'

She had two men looking at her as if she were speaking Swahili and she was close to tears. They didn't understand and she had to leave before she disintegrated.

She snagged her gorgeous new bag—ten bucks

at the charity shop…who'd have thought it?—and tried desperately to sound sensible.

'I'll leave you to your very important discussion,' she told them. 'How to accommodate a child without letting him interfere with your lives. I'll head back to the apartment to fetch my stuff but then I'm leaving. I'll assure Peggy that McLellan Place is fine as a place to live but I'll also tell her…beware where she gives her heart. She's already given it to Henry and that's a safe bet because Henry loves her back. Peggy's preparing to cross the world for love, change her life, put everything she has on the line. I don't think either of you are capable of doing that.'

And then, because she couldn't help herself, she took a step forward, stood on her toes and kissed Matt. Lightly on the lips but moving away fast.

'I think… I hope there's a plane leaving this afternoon,' she told him. 'If there is I'll be on it. No, don't leave, you two have important things to discuss and none of them involve me. Thanks for the compliment, Matt. Thanks for giving me an amazing few days. I'll remember them all my life. Goodbye…and good luck. Please, don't follow.'

And she swiped away an angry tear and headed out.

Steven's voice followed.

'They're all like that,' he was saying. 'Emotional creatures. Time of the month? Who knows? I've been married three times and I've never figured it out. But it's okay, I can approve your adoption without her. You don't really need to marry on Henry's account.'

He couldn't follow. He had enough sense to realise that following her and reasoning on a packed New York pavement was never going to work.

There was also the bill for the business lunch. Steven seemed to realise the gravity of the situation—maybe he was even enjoying it—but he wasn't about to let Matt go without paying his half. Meg therefore had a five-minute start on him, and the traffic closed in. By the time he got back to his apartment she'd used her headstart to good effect. Her things were gone. She was gone.

Doing a romantic rush to the airport wasn't his

style but he found he had no choice. He checked the website and learned there was a flight leaving midafternoon. But she'd moved fast. By the time he reached the airport she was already through international security.

'The only way through is if you buy yourself a ticket,' the security guard said jovially, and Matt almost decided to take him up on it.

He didn't have his passport on him. He had nothing apart from the memories of Meg's pale face. Of a last kiss.

He was forced to stop and think. What had just happened?

He'd put a loaded gun to her head.

Had he no sense?

He'd told Steven he'd hoped they'd marry before she'd agreed. More, he'd somehow linked that proposal to Steven's agreement for Henry's care.

He'd spoken in anger and in haste, pushed by Steven's coldness. That haste had had him making assumptions.

He knew Meg was falling in love with him. She'd said so. She'd already offered to share her life with Henry. He'd just put everything together, too fast.

He was an astute businessman. He knew how

to negotiate a contract and it wasn't by bullying. It had been anger with Steven that had had jolted him from being sensible, from taking things calmly.

Where to go from here?

He could head back to the office, work until tomorrow and then take a flight that'd have him with her with only a twenty-four-hour gap. Or he could hire his own jet.

But would it make a difference?

He stared at massive metal doors, shut tight. Meg would be boarding.

Had she used the open first-class ticket he'd bought her when she came? He hoped so. He'd given her the ticket so she didn't feel trapped.

And then he'd tried to trap her. Ready-made family. Ready-made wife.

Reality was setting in now, cold as the metal doors in front of him. Meg had talked of her work, the things she did to make a living.

They're what I do. They're not who I am.

Family? It wasn't what he did.

Loving? He obviously hadn't a clue how to do that, either.

He thought suddenly of a time long ago, his parents heading for vacation, and Matt desperate to go, too. He must have been…maybe five?

So young it was just a blur. But when he'd seen his parents' suitcases in the hall he'd raced to get his backpack, and in a fit of inspiration he'd popped his toy squirrel—Eric—into his mother's capacious purse. Eric was precious. He had to be in the safest place possible.

And then…he remembered his mother telling him to be a big boy, he was staying home with nanny. There'd been a swift kiss from her, an appalled look from his father—yeah, he'd been sobbing—and they were gone.

His nanny at the time—Elspeth—had been one of the better ones, kind and almost as appalled as he'd been when he'd calmed down enough to realise that Eric had gone, too. She'd known how precious Eric was and she'd taken the almost-unbelievable step of bundling him into a cab and following his parents to the airport.

To metal doors like this one. To an official who'd said he'd see what he could do to get a message to them—but Eric was gone.

Six weeks later his parents had returned but Eric hadn't come home with them.

Home… Where was home anyway? Surely he needed to be over the concept by now?

His phone pinged in his jacket. He took it out and stared at the screen.

Helen. Work.

That's what I am.

'Anything else I can help you with, sir?' the security guard asked. Obviously a lone business-man staring blindly at a closed door needed to be moved on.

'I… No. Thank you.'

He'd been dumb. He'd pushed her too hard, too fast, but a part of him knew what had just happened was inevitable.

He'd tried to *do* family. Meg had told him that was impossible.

So now what?

He clicked Recall on his phone.

'Helen?'

He needed to get back to what he was.

Once again she was ensconced in first-class luxury. She'd considered trading her open ticket for economy but they wouldn't give her a refund and she'd decided, what the heck? A few more hours of luxury and then back to real life.

She'd just thrown away a life that was pure fantasy.

She donned her first-class pyjamas and the

flight attendant was instantly on hand to offer to make up her bed. 'But wouldn't you like dinner first?' she asked. 'We can offer a seven-course degustation menu. And would madam like champagne?'

Madam wouldn't, and flight attendants were trained to read nuances. She offered to dim the lights and left Meg to sleep.

Meg shoved her pillow on top of her head and thought, *What have I done?*

She'd given up on Matt.

'Maybe I could have changed him,' she whispered to her pillow. 'Maybe if I married him he'd be a different person. He'd learn to be family.'

Right. She thought suddenly of advice her grandma had given her long ago. It was a joke. Sort of. *Brides can go into marriage thinking, Aisle, altar, hymn. It won't happen, Meg, love. Look long and hard before you leap.*

She hadn't looked long, but she had looked hard.

'He'd break my heart,' she whispered into her muffling pillow. 'I'd sit at that great mansion watching Henry grow up, watching Peggy grow old, waiting for snippets, flying visits from a man who says he loves me. I might even have to watch Henry turn into the same, a man who doesn't have a clue what love's about.

'I could teach them both.

'There you go again. Aisle. Altar. Hymn. Get a grip. You've made a wise decision. You know he'd break your heart.

'I know that,' she told the pillow. 'So why do I feel like my heart's already breaking?'

CHAPTER THIRTEEN

PEGGY AND HENRY arrived at McLellan Place two months later, and by Christmas they'd settled in. Peggy made a warm, if rather muddled, attempt at being all the family Henry needed. Matt put supports in place to keep them safe and content. Even though he'd thought he'd visit every couple of weeks, he found himself there almost every weekend, increasingly taking work with him so he could extend his stay.

Because Henry needed him? Maybe not, but he was always so joyful to see him that the effort to get there seemed minor.

Peggy and Henry fished, beachcombed, turned the place into a sort of home.

He'd talked Steven out of the idea of Henry following his father to boarding school. Instead he started at the local school and seemed to fit in.

Then Christmas.

Christmas for Matt was usually a duty to be

got over as fast as possible. There'd be a McLellan family dinner at New York's latest on-trend restaurant, with assorted relations all trying to outdo each other by revealing how much insider gossip they'd gleaned about each other in the previous year.

This year he didn't hear any of it.

Somewhat reluctantly he'd invited his mother to McLellan Place, but of course, she declined. It was as if he'd invited her to share a bad smell.

'You have a child there now?' she said with disdain. 'The son of that sleazy Steven Walker? And the child's grandmother, too? What business is it of yours?'

He'd made it his business, but on Christmas Day the place still felt empty.

He thought, If Meg were here, she'd have hauled Christmas dinner into the snug. She might also have scorned the massive Christmas tree his staff had organised. Plus the turkey. The roasted bird was carried into the dining room and Henry stared at it in wonder, while Peggy snorted as she saw its size.

'We'll be eating leftovers for ever.'

'I like turkey sandwiches,' Matt said weakly.

'I bet it's wasted.' Peggy was getting more and more acerbic as she became secure. 'Like all these bedrooms. They're for show, that's what they are. No one's used the whole west wing since we've been here. Not that we're ungrateful,' she amended hurriedly. 'It's a lovely place to live.'

'I liked your island as much,' Henry told her as he gamely tackled his turkey. He'd settled well into living here, revelling in his grandma's devotion and Matt's frequent visits. 'My friend Robbie at school says this place is like an island. It's like everything is blocked out. Robbie says the spikes on our gates make his mum feel scared.' He surveyed the tiny indent they'd made in the giant bird with concern. 'Matt, I don't think I like turkey sandwiches.'

'Neither do I,' Peggy told him.

'But I do like Meg.' Henry suddenly sounded wistful. 'I wish she could have come for Christmas.' He brightened. 'I'm calling her this afternoon. I want to show her the pictures of the shells Grandma and I found.'

'You're calling Meg?' he said. Why did that make something in his chest lurch?

'At four o'clock,' Henry told him. 'Grandma said that'd be a good time.'

It'd be a good time for them, Matt thought. It'd

be the morning after Christmas in Rowan Bay. They'd have missed Meg's Christmas.

Had Meg been alone for Christmas?

He thought of her in that ramshackle old house. It did have a shiny new roof—he'd organised it—but had she been alone? He kept remembering the words she'd used when she'd invited Peggy and Henry to share her home.

I'll get to come home after a day's charter and the lights will be on.

By bringing Henry here, he'd taken that from her.

When the adoption came through he'd be able to take Henry back for a visit, he thought, but then, it wouldn't make much difference. She'd still be alone.

Peggy and Henry went back to tackling their turkey but Matt had lost his appetite. He glanced around at the truly impressive dining room. The dining table was all elegance, crimson and gold, with the gleaming mahogany table surface shining through.

To give his staff their due, they'd also tried to make it child-friendly. The decorations contained strings of sparkly Santas, and the centrepiece was a revolving Santa's workshop, complete with beavering elves. The Christmas tree was tasteful, exquisite. The food arriving from the kitchen was amazing.

Christmas at its best? It still felt lonely.

'Do you remember the fish Meg cooked in seaweed?' Henry asked and Matt flinched. He remembered. If he could turn back time…

He couldn't. Meg had made her choice. She didn't want this lifestyle and he couldn't force her.

But if she was in Rowan Bay by herself… If she was as lonely as he was…

What the…? He wasn't lonely. What was he thinking?

But if there was a chance she'd changed her mind…

'Maybe I could talk to her, too,' he told Henry, trying to sound as if it didn't matter. He'd spoken to Meg since she'd left but the calls had been brief. Working out travel for Peggy and Henry. Organising her promised roof. Giving updates on Henry. Nothing personal.

'Do you want to say Happy Christmas?' Henry asked, and Matt nodded.

'I do.'

What else did he have to say?

Are you lonely? Will you change your mind?

He wouldn't say it, he thought, but he would say Happy Christmas and see where the conversation led.

It was eight in the morning, Boxing Day, and Meg's beach was packed with Nippers as far as the eye could see.

Nippers were kids who'd be Australia's next generation of lifeguards, or simply beach-safe adults. Rowan Bay kids loved the organisation and the training it embraced. Parents and grandparents loved it, too. As soon as Christmas was done, every kid within a coo-ee of Rowan Beach transformed into a yellow-and-red Nipper.

The wind had been forecast to blow from the west and strengthen, which meant the main Rowan Bay beach would be choppy. The beach in front of Meg's house was a sheltered easterly cove, so the entire function had thus been shifted and given an early start.

There was a row of portable toilets by the chook pen. A water tanker was hooked to a shower to allow kids to be sluiced. Rows of barbecues, manned by an army of parents wearing fundraising Nipper aprons, were producing breakfast, and the smell of bacon was drifting across the beach to where Meg was sitting in the shallows.

'Meg!' Maureen, her next-door neighbour, was wearing a pink swimming costume and a life vest. She'd been helping Meg supervise the splashing competition for the toddlers, and had taken a break for some much-needed morning coffee. Now she'd returned, holding Meg's phone. 'Your phone? Thought so. It's ringing. Your turn for a break.'

It'd be Henry. Drat, she'd almost missed him.

She loved their calls. Somehow it still seemed important that she be a part of his life. It still seemed important that Henry be part of hers.

They video-called most days, talking of nothing and everything. School. What he'd found on the beach. What sort of fish the guys she took out on the charters had caught that day. Even trivial stuff like the new type of chocolate-chip cookie Matt's cook had made.

'What's your cook's name?' Meg had asked and Henry had hesitated before answering.

'Her name's Esther but I'm not supposed to know,' he'd told her. 'Matt says don't disturb the staff. It's better that way.'

'Really?' That had been a gut clencher. If she were there…

She wasn't there. She'd walked away from being part of Henry's life, of Matt's life.

Her life was here and life was okay. She shook herself free of seawater and took the phone from Maureen.

'Henry?'

'It's Matt,' the voice on the other end of the line said. 'Happy Christmas.'

Matt. It was almost a month since she'd talked to him. It was almost—what?—ten minutes since she'd thought of him.

'H-happy Christmas.' He still had the power to take her breath away. 'I… Thank you.' And then her breath caught. This was Henry's phone. 'Is anything wrong?'

'Nothing's wrong,' he said quickly. 'Henry was about to phone when his new puppy escaped with the Christmas beanie Peggy's knitted for him. It has a red pompom on top and if that's not asking for trouble I don't know what is. Peggy and Henry are currently chasing one cocker spaniel puppy across the lawn. Stretchie's helping. I don't like the beanie's chances.'

'Oh…' she gasped and then choked on laughter. 'A puppy. What a gorgeous idea. Was that your Christmas gift to him?'

'It was,' he told her. 'Made more complicated by Henry's insistence that Christmas gifts aren't given until after Christmas pudding. It's very hard to hide a puppy until after pudding.'

'I bet it is. Well done, you. Did Esther help?'

'Esther?'

'Your cook,' she told him. 'Henry says she's great.'

'She did help,' he said cautiously. 'Henry told you about Esther?'

'He did, and also about your edict about not getting to know the staff. What's that about?' She was standing knee deep in the shallows, surveying her Nippers, and she was feeling strange. Commenting on Matt's lifestyle? She had no right, but strangely it felt appropriate.

'If you get to know the staff it hurts when they leave,' Matt said and that was enough to give her pause. To make her think.

'Is that what you learned?' she said. 'When you were a kid?'

'It doesn't… We weren't talking about me.'

'I guess that's not what you phoned to talk about,' she agreed. 'It doesn't fit inside the Matt McLellan boundaries.'

'Meg...'

'Sorry.' She sighed. 'That was uncalled for. It's not my business. You'd have thought I'd have learned by now. Are you having a good Christmas?'

'We are.'

'Who's there?'

'Peggy and Henry.'

'Not Steven?'

'He sent Henry a very expensive construction kit.'

'Bully for Steven. He gets boundaries, too.'

'Do you need to sound so cynical?'

She caught herself. 'Sorry. I don't mean to. It's just a different way of life from the one I'm used to.'

'So who did you share Christmas with?' he said, and she heard a trace of cynicism in *his* voice. Like 'pot calling the kettle black' cynicism.

'Lots of people,' she said diffidently.

'Really?'

And that had her arcing up. She knew criticism when she heard it.

'Really,' she snapped. 'I'm not dependent on Matt McLellan for company. Maureen came over for Christmas morning eggnog. Then we had a massive barbecue on the beach. Maureen's kids and grandkids. Two of the charter boat guys. Charlie's ex-wife and her new husband—she's done so much better than Charlie. Their kids. And food… The best seafood ever. You might have a professional cook, but we can catch crayfish half an hour from our front door. And pavlova. There are raspberries on Maureen's bushes and one of her kids has a cow. Fresh cream. Beat that, Matt McLellan.'

'I guess I can't,' he said weakly. 'It sounds great.'

'It was great.'

'So you're not lonely?'

'How can I be lonely?' She stood in the shallows and looked around her, at the community she loved, at the community she was part of.

'Matt, this is a video call,' she told him. 'Can you turn your camera on?'

And she flicked the video icon on her phone and turned the camera to the scene around her.

Maureen was in the water covered with toddlers. A bunch of learner bodyboarders were in the shallows. Older Nippers were organised into swimming races around buoys set further out. Mums and dads talked or snoozed on the beach. Boof was digging a hole to China with a couple of other dogs helping.

She turned her phone to show her feet in the water and she kicked, a splash that was pretty much defiance.

'These are my people,' she said. 'I'm having fun.'

'I didn't ask that, though,' Matt said slowly. 'Meg, I asked if you're lonely.'

Oh, help. Heaven preserve her from a perceptive male.

'I'm less lonely than I would be at McLellan Place,' she told him. 'Being a part-time wife.'

'Meg, I love you.'

There went her breath again. How was she expected to breathe when he said things like that?

I love you.

Why was he saying it now?

'How can you say that when you have all those boundaries?' she managed. 'You can't just love at weekends. It doesn't work like that.'

Silence.

He'd turned his camera on as well, and she could see him. It was almost like talking face-to-face. Matt was dressed for Christmas in winter, in a crimson sweater and classy trousers. His dark hair was neat, beautifully groomed.

She was dressed for messy Christmas in summer. Bikini. Salt water. Not a lot else.

She swiped a dripping curl from her forehead. Matt looked… Matt looked.

Focus on boundaries, she told herself. She needed to think of them. She couldn't live with them, no matter how sexy this guy looked. No matter how much her heart lurched every time she saw him.

'Some boundaries are necessary,' Matt said at last. 'Meg, you know I'm happy to share. I wouldn't have boundaries with you.'

'But you'd keep those gates locked. You'd advise me not to get to know your cook.'

'It works.'

'Not for me it doesn't.' She turned her camera back to the splashy toddlers. 'This is fun. Where's the fun for you, Matt McLellan?'

'I want you.' It was a guttural response, almost primeval in its intensity. It made her take a step back. It almost made her click Disconnect.

Why? Because it evoked an answer in her that was stronger than any echo.

I want you.

She looked at her screen, into his dark, troubled eyes, and she thought it was just as well she was on the other side of the world. If he were here, if he were to take her into his arms...

He wouldn't. Or maybe he would, but only if it fitted into the time slots he had available.

'I know you do,' she managed at last. Maureen was looking up from where she was crouched in the shallows with their splashing toddlers. Seeing her distress? She needed to finish this conversation and get back to what really mattered. Rowan Bay Boxing Day. Community. Life.

'It's the best compliment I've ever been paid,' she whispered. 'You loving me. But it won't work. Not while you don't know your cook's name.'

'I do know her name.'

'You know what I mean.'

'Meg...'

'Give my love to Henry,' she said sadly. 'And to Peggy. Tell Henry I'll head inside and ring him at about seven tonight, your time. I need to see his puppy. Will you be staying with him for much longer?'

'Until New Year. Meg, what do you expect me to do? I can't—'

'I don't expect you to do anything,' she told him. 'I understand. There's nothing either of us can do. I love you, Matt, but there's the problem.

You have your boundaries you can't cross, and I can't cross them, either.'

He stared at the blank screen. Then he swore and shoved the phone onto the table so hard it slid across the shining surface and landed on the floor beyond.

Then he thought, uh-oh, that was Henry's phone.

Thankfully, it wasn't broken.

If it'd been his, would he have cared?

Of course he would. His phone was his link to his world. Those days at sea when he'd been out of contact had been a disaster. At least one multimillion-dollar contract had fallen over because of it.

But he'd been with Meg.

He stared down at the blank screen of Henry's phone and the thing almost mocked him. Two minutes ago it had been filled with life, with laughter. With Meg.

If he'd used his own high-tech phone he could have recorded. He could be playing it back right now.

He could be showing himself pictures of a woman who was nothing to do with him, of a life he wasn't part of.

He stood, silent, letting his thoughts go where they willed.

Outside Henry and Peggy were engaged in a silly game with Stretchie and the yet-unnamed puppy. They were rolling on the grass.

It was December. The grass was wet. They'd be soaked.

Peggy wouldn't care. All she wanted was for her grandson to be happy. He watched her giggling with Henry, and he thought, *She's shed ten years.*

She'd abandoned her island. She'd abandoned her life to keep her grandson happy.

He'd asked Meg to do the same and she'd refused.

The screen was still blank. He closed his eyes and it was filled again, with Meg, with a beach crowded with kids, dogs, laughter. Life.

Meg.

Their conversation was being replayed. A repetitive loop.

And suddenly the loop seemed to tighten, focusing on two statements.

I asked if you're lonely.

I'm less lonely than I would be at McLellan Place. Being a part-time wife.

That was an admission, he thought. She *was* lonely.

So what? It didn't mean she was missing him.

But if it did? How could he persuade her...?

He couldn't. She'd made her decision. She couldn't fit into his lifestyle.

The thought of her was still with him, the sight of her splashing in the shallows.

Meg.

He wanted her.

The feeling was suddenly a hunger so vast he had to open his eyes and steady himself. His foundations seemed to be disappearing, leaving him foundering.

And it wasn't just Meg.

He stared back out of the window. It was almost dark and starting to rain, just drizzle but enough for sensible people to run for cover. Henry and Peggy hadn't noticed. They were entranced, having fun, not caring about minor details such as wet clothes.

Peggy... Seventy-six years old.

The only thing she'd care about was if she lost Henry, he thought. She'd do anything to prevent that, and he'd help her. Once the adoption went through they'd be safe together.

So he was fighting for Henry and Peggy.

What about Meg?

He thought back to what she'd said. *You have your boundaries.*

Who didn't? He had to have boundaries to survive.

Peggy didn't have boundaries.

And neither did Meg, he conceded. She'd opened her home, opened her heart to Peggy and Henry. He had no doubt that if Steven hadn't intervened that was where Peggy and Henry would be. Sharing Christmas at Rowan Bay.

That was where he wanted to be.

Not possible.

Why not?

For a million reasons, he thought.

Name them.

Right. First, Steven would never agree. Steven had met the idea of adoption with initial consent, but Matt knew that a part of his reaction to his small son was his need for public approval. The story of Amanda's death and Steven's surprise parentage had filtered through the circles they moved in. Denying responsibility didn't fit Steven's self-image. Nor would sending Henry to Australia. If it was hinted at, the adoption would be off.

It couldn't be done.

So... Taking Peggy and Henry to Rowan Bay was problematic.

But him?

Taking himself to Rowan Bay?

What would he do with himself? His business was here. His life was here.

And then he thought, *Is business what I do or what I am?*

It was Meg's question, an accusation, echoing back to haunt him.

He looked again at Peggy and Henry. They were self-contained, gloriously happy with their dogs and their new life. They'd been delighted to see him when he'd arrived last night, they'd been even more delighted when he'd said he was staying for a week, but they didn't need him. Neither of them had invited him outside with them. They'd be expecting him to return to his office, as he normally did when he was here.

They wouldn't expect him to roll on wet grass.

Even if he did...it wasn't who he was.

Who was he?

What was important to him?

It wasn't a question he'd ever asked himself.

So ask it now.

This place was important to him, he conceded, this sheltered headland, this untouched beach. He'd fight for it.

This house? He looked around at the glamorous interior and conceded...not so much.

Peggy and Henry?

He glanced again at the pair outside and thought, yes, they'd become part of who he was. He'd fight for them, with every means at his disposal.

And his business? The massive financial world he lived in? He'd been bred to it. Its care had been ingrained from such an early age that he'd never questioned it.

Why?

Was it what he *was*?

The McLellan's foundation did so much good. It employed so many. The thought of it crumbling was unthinkable.

It didn't impress Meg.

And there she was again, front and centre. Meg.

He couldn't go to her. She wouldn't stay with him.

And then he paused as he heard the thought bubble.

She wouldn't stay with him.

But he hadn't asked her to stay with him. He'd asked her to fit in around the edges of what he was.

Of what he did.

Maybe Meg could be a part of who he *was*?

He closed his eyes again, letting his thoughts drift, to Meg as he'd just seen her, to a laughing, beautiful woman who'd taken the life she'd been given and accepted it with love and courage.

She'd been falling in love with him. She'd said it, but she couldn't love within his boundaries.

His world was shifting. *Boundaries.* Where were they and what was he protecting?

Himself?

A sudden flash of insight had him remembering Nanny Elspeth and the gardener who'd been sacked when he was small. He remembered the grief, the emptiness.

'That's what you're afraid of.' He said it out loud.

But then he glanced outside again, at Peggy, who'd taken herself off to her island in her own emptiness.

And Henry…

My friend Robbie at school says this place is like an island.

His world felt as if it were shifting.

Boundaries...

The French doors were suddenly flung open and a soaking Peggy and Henry and two sodden dogs burst into the room. Water scattered all over the parquet floor.

His parents would have had kittens.

But they're boundaries, he told himself as Henry launched himself at him, bursting with excitement.

'I'm going to call her Puddles because she loves splashing,' he said excitedly. 'She likes getting her nose wet. I bet she loves the beach.'

He thought suddenly of the turtles, of the nesting sites. That was how they were protected, with boundaries.

Or you figured another way.

'We'll need to train her to protect the turtle nesting sites,' he found himself saying. 'And not to chase the birds. We'll need to watch her until she's trained.' And then he thought, *We?*

He couldn't train a dog at weekends.

How many boundaries needed to disappear?

'I'm good at watching,' Henry said happily.

'She's a smart dog.' And suddenly he wrapped his skinny, soggy arms around Matt's body and Matt found he was lifting one small boy into his arms and holding. Hugging. Feeling Henry's small body cradle to his, his face nestle into his neck.

Feeling boundaries start to crack.

And then it was done. Henry struggled to get down and whooped off toward the kitchen to tell Esther the news about Puddles's new name. Esther. Not 'the cook'.

Another boundary.

Matt looked up and found Peggy watching. Smiling.

'Feels good, doesn't it?' she asked and he thought he saw tears behind her smile.

'It surely does. Happy Christmas, Peggy. You might need to go dry off before you freeze to death.'

'I'd die happy,' she said and he knew she would.

'Peggy…'

'Mmm?'

'I know I said I'd stay until New Year.'

Her smile faltered a little and then recovered. 'You can't? It's okay. Henry and I are okay.'

'You are okay,' he told her. 'But I want you…

I want *us* to be more okay. I'm thinking of taking a fast trip to Australia.'

'To find Meg?'

'To ask her to marry me,' he said, because why not lay it on the line?

'She wouldn't have you last time,' Peggy said simply and he thought how much did Peggy see? 'So what's changed?'

'I think I have.'

Her eyes searched his face and slowly her smile returned.

'Is that anything to do with the way Henry hugged you?'

'Sort of,' he told her and then, because it seemed important, he stepped forward and hugged her, too. An all-enveloping, lifting hug that made her squeal, that had Henry tearing back from the kitchen to see what was happening.

'You're cuddling Grandma,' he said in astonishment, and Matt set the blushing, giggling Peggy down and hugged Henry again for good measure.

'I'm practising,' he told Henry. 'I'd never figured out that hugs are important but now… Maybe they're the most important things in the world.'

'Puddles likes hugs,' Henry said. 'Though she chews my ear when I hug her tight.'

'You might need to put up with chewing for a hug,' Matt told him. 'A chewed ear seems a small price to pay. I'm about to confess that all sorts of things can disappear if a hug is the pay-off. Peggy...'

'You go get 'em,' Peggy said happily. 'You said you'd stay here until New Year? Henry and I can sacrifice that for a very big pay-off indeed.'

CHAPTER FOURTEEN

CHRISTMAS IN AUSTRALIA meant the start of summer holidays, and holidays meant Charlie's charters were booked solid. The weather was great and the fishing was perfect. Meg cleaned and gutted more fish than she could count.

Thursday morning's charter was due to leave at eight, late for a charter. The fishing was usually better at dawn but she wasn't complaining.

She and Boof arrived to find the jetty almost deserted. The rest of the boats were already out. Her boat was tied at the docks. She was a sturdier vessel than the not-lamented *Bertha*.

No one was queued and waiting.

Cancellation? Her heart sank. A cancellation meant no pay, but she headed into the office and found Charlie beaming.

'The punter's already on board.'

'Punter?' she said cautiously. 'One?'

'That's right.'

It had happened before—one cashed-up tourist wanting sole attention. Usually she steered clear. Being alone on a boat with someone she didn't know was risky.

'Why didn't you get one of the guys to take it?'

'Specific request for you,' Charlie told her. 'Repeat customer so it's okay. Enjoy yourself.'

'Charlie...' She glowered. 'If it's some sleaze, I'm getting right off.'

'Suit yourself,' he said happily. 'With the rate this guy's prepared to pay I might even be tempted to take the boat out myself. Go check him out and let me know.'

Right. She headed out into the morning sunshine thinking at least it was a great day for being at sea, and with one customer there'd be fewer fish to clean.

She stepped on board—and Matt appeared from below.

Matt.

Boof went nuts.

Boof was far too well behaved to be permitted to go nuts. She should click her fingers, order him back to her side.

How could she do anything? Her heart seemed to have stopped.

Matt was catching Boof's paws as he jumped up. Fondling his ears.

He was dressed casually in neat chinos, boat shoes and an open-necked shirt.

Why did he look different?

To be honest she wasn't capable of wondering much at all. All she knew was that Matt was here and she was having trouble jump-starting her heart again.

'Happy New Year,' he told her, smiling straight at her.

'I… Happy New Year.'

'I wanted to come earlier but I had things to organise.'

'Really?'

'Really.'

'I… You've come all this way…' She was struggling here. 'Henry? Peggy?'

'They're still at McLellan Place. I'd have brought them but Steven still won't let Henry leave the country. Not until the adoption goes through.'

'You're still…adopting?' Each word seemed an effort.

'It's early days yet,' he told her. 'But as long as it's made clear publicly that Steven hasn't abandoned Henry, he's amenable. But meanwhile, Meg, I've paid for charter. You want to put to sea?'

She took three deep breaths and steadied.

'Where do you want to go?'

'Garnett Island,' he told her. 'I need to check my new investment.'

'You've bought it?' That was a squeak. 'From Peggy?'

'I have.'

'But why?'

'Let's go see,' he told her. 'We can talk about it later. It's a great day. Let's just enjoy it.'

'Matt...'

'There are lots of things we need to talk about,' he said, suddenly grave. 'There are so many things I messed up. I need time to explain, time to get things in perspective. If you'll trust me to go to sea with you... Meg, can we enjoy the morning and let things happen as they will? No rush. For now let's just be together and let the future take care of itself.'

There was little choice but to agree. In truth there was little to disagree about. He wanted to go to Garnett and she was being paid to take him. What was there in that to make her feel as if the world were holding its breath?

There were so many questions spinning in her head but there didn't seem any way she could get them out. Matt didn't seem to want to talk, so neither did she.

She stood at the wheel and he stood beside her. Not touching but close.

The day was calm and warm—he really was seeing Bass Strait at its best. Dolphins were treating their wake as their own personal surf, leaping in and out of the milky foam, ducking under the boat, charging ahead—like a guard of honour?

It was almost dreamlike. That Matt was here... She had no idea what was happening but the closer they got to Garnett, the more she felt that something had stilled within her, some emptiness was filling.

It had to be her imagination. There was a part of her that was fighting to keep her stupid heart under control.

He'd bought Garnett? So what? It wouldn't dent his wealth and it'd give Peggy independence. It was only sensible that he come and check it out, figure what to do with it.

With her. He'd asked for her.

Down, she told her heart. Stop jumping about like a puppy with a treat in store. She had to stay sensible.

Halfway out she produced her standard punter

fare of cheese sandwiches and coffee. She stayed at the wheel, munching her sandwich, checking out a bunch of cormorants diving off one of the rocky outcrops.

'It's stunning,' Matt said softly. 'I never realised how beautiful. Last time I was here...'

'You were too busy working out how to stay alive,' she said dryly and he smiled.

'I didn't have to worry about that. You were showing us how to live.'

There was enough in that to take her breath away all over again. There was also enough there to make her focus—fiercely—on her cheese sandwich and not say anything at all.

Finally Garnett Island came into view. As far as she knew, no one had been near the place for months. There'd been a couple of decent storms since they'd last been here. Peggy's boat hadn't fared so well. It was still at its mooring, but it had started taking water and was now partly submerged.

'That'll be a job, getting rid of her,' Matt said.

'You'll replace her?'

'I can't stay on the island without a decent boat.'

What the...? 'You intend to stay on the island?'

'I hope so. It's a great place for a family holiday. And Peggy tells me it's a haven for sea creatures. I'm starting to think we might form a chain of wildlife sanctuaries. Small but many. Today, McLellan Place and Garnett Island. Tomorrow, the world.'

There was even more to take her breath away. Luckily she had stuff to do. It took skill to manoeuvre the boat safely into the only part of Peggy's jetty that was still available. Matt helped, stepping easily out of the boat, manoeuvring ropes, attaching them with skill.

This was a charter. He'd wanted to come here to see his purchase. She had to stay sensible.

'I'll stay with the boat,' she said and he grinned.

'You think I engineered this whole thing so I could sit up in Peggy's house by myself? In your dreams, Meg O'Hara. What you see before you is step one of the McLellan and O'Hara Master Plan, and that plan has Meg O'Hara right in the very middle. Take you away and the whole thing disintegrates. You want to see?' And he held out his hand to help her off the boat.

She stared at his hand in bewilderment.

No one helped her off her boat. For some reason that thought was front and centre. Not since she could remember. Even as a tiny kid she'd made that leap herself.

He held out his hand and she thought, *I can do it myself.*

But... The McLellan and O'Hara Master Plan. Not the McLellan Plan.

His hand was just there.

She reached out and took it. He tugged her upward and she came a little too fast. It turned into a hug, a gentle caress, and then he put her away, still holding her hand but taking it no further. As if there were things to be said. Things to be sorted.

'If we're going up to the house maybe we should take the sandwiches,' she ventured. 'The charter includes food for the day. Cheese sandwiches for morning tea, salad sandwiches for lunch, fruit cake for a midafternoon snack.'

'Food's been organised,' he said. 'It's in the house. Come and see.'

His hold on her hand firmed. Numbly, she allowed him to lead her along the overgrown path, up to the house.

Boof, delighted to be off the boat, hared away to rediscover what seemed a doggy paradise.

Last time Meg had been here this hadn't seemed a human paradise. It had looked sad.

Now, though, the little cottage almost gleamed a welcome. Loose tin on the roof had been nailed down. Someone had worked on the garden. A pile of weeds were heaped by the fence, as if waiting to be composted.

'We had to work fast,' Matt said placidly. 'Do you realise how hard it is to get things done in Australia between Christmas and New Year?'

'It's beach and sleep time here,' she managed, feeling stunned. 'But, Matt, why...?'

And then he opened the door to the cottage and she couldn't say another word.

Gone was the appalling settee with the broken springs, the threadbare rugs, the rickety furniture. Peggy had asked for the things she most valued to be taken off the island and Meg had expected to see the place stripped. Instead, the shabby furniture had been replaced by... gorgeous.

No, not gorgeous, she thought, as she stared in amazement around the little living room. By simple. By comfortable. By cosy.

The settee was big and squishy. The rug was thick and warm. Lamps were set on either side of the fireplace.

Some of Peggy's photographs had been returned to the mantle. Another photograph took pride of place, though. It was a picture taken by the reporter from Rowan Bay's local paper the day they were rescued.

Four people were climbing from the helicopter. Peggy was holding Henry. She was turning back to smile as Matt lifted Meg from the chopper.

It was an action photo but it was much more. It was four people who'd come together in the most extraordinary circumstances.

'I figure it's our first family photo,' Matt said tentatively. 'At least I hope it is.'

She stared at the photo and then she turned and stared at Matt.

He'd lost his assurance, she thought. His eyes held doubt. Hope. Fear?

'What's happening?' she managed.

'Meg, we have a chance to change our lives,' he said and he took her hands. The link was warm, strong, but still she felt the tremor of uncertainty. 'I've messed it up. I'm hoping with everything I have that I haven't messed it up for ever.'

How to answer that? She had to make her voice work. *Caution*, her sensible self was saying. *If it's more of the same, you have to find the strength to pull away.*

'You'd better… You'd better tell me.'

'First things first.' She was right, the look in his eyes was definitely anxious. 'I've resigned as chairman of McLellan Corporation.'

'You've resigned.'

'As of this week. My combined family's currently having forty fits. My cousins are vying for the job. I have the biggest pecuniary interest so I get the say. I'm actually thinking of appointing my secretary. Helen knows the company backward and she'll support what I plan.'

'What you plan?' Did she sound like a parrot? She couldn't care.

'Here's the thing,' he told her. 'Meg, after Christmas, after your phone call, after seeing you on the beach, I started thinking why am I doing…what I'm doing. The answer came back that I'm good at it. I'm good at moving and shaking. I'm good at making money. But you're right, it's what I do. I've never questioned what I am. So then I thought who am I? And the deeper question is, who do I want to be?'

'Which is?' She'd started to shake. Why? It was warm enough.

Someone must have been here this morning. There was a fire in the grate. She could see the table set in the kitchen. She could see a bottle of wine. Glasses.

To say she was discombobulated was an understatement. All she could do was feel the warmth of Matt's hold, and wait for him…to set her world right?

'That's where the adoption comes in,' he told her. 'I want to *be* Henry's dad. I want to *be* a part of his life.'

'That's…that's great?'

'And I want to care for Peggy. We've talked about it. We reckon if I'm Henry's dad, then Peggy can be my mother-in-law. It makes sense. We both like the idea.'

'I… Yeah.' She could see that.

'And I don't want to work in Manhattan any more. At least, not much. Meg, as soon as I started thinking past what I do, the "wants" and the "don't wants" started cascading. When I was fifteen my grandfather allocated me the office next to his. He introduced me to "our people". As a kid, as a college student, I'd use my over-the-top office to study, picking up knowledge of the company while I did. It seemed natural. It seemed what I was. It's only this jolt… It's only you, Meg O'Hara, who's made me see it's not who I am at all.'

'So…' Wow, she was struggling. 'You're adopting Henry—and Peggy? You're quitting work?'

'I'm not quitting work. I'm probably going to be busier than I've ever been. That's the next step. I asked myself what gives me the most satisfaction. And one of the things is my turtles.'

'Protecting them…'

'With my gates? No. I've figured another way. I'm throwing the gates open. Peggy concurs. She'll help me. We're starting to channel McLellan money into forming conservation areas. More, we'll make part of what we do education. McLellan Place is one of the best places in the world to bring school groups, to teach, to learn. And we can set up places all around the world.'

'W-we?'

'You and me,' he told her. 'This isn't who I want to be, Meg O'Hara. It's what I want us to be. Which is you and me and Peggy and Henry and Boof and Stretchie and Puddles and whoever else comes along. My family.'

'Family.' She felt dizzy. This was unreal. Crazy. She was frantically trying to make herself make sense.

'How can you bring school groups to Garnett?' she managed, which was ridiculous but her head was spinning in so many directions the dizziness was almost making her sway.

'We might have trouble bringing school groups here,' he conceded, and he smiled down at her, a wide, encompassing smile that made her heart turn over. 'It's definitely a conservation area but I'm thinking we might be a little bit selfish.'

'What…what do you mean?'

'Let me show you,' he said, and his dark eyes gleamed with laughter. And tenderness. And… something that made her feel as if she were melt-ing.

And before she knew what he was about he'd swept her into his arms and carried her up the stairs.

There were three bedrooms up here: Peggy's, the little room she'd furnished for Henry and a spare. In the time she'd been here, Meg had in-vestigated and seen a barren room with nothing to recommend it but sunbeams shining through a dormer window and a view almost to Tasma-nia.

But now the room had been transformed with soft rugs, chintz curtains, lamps. Centre stage was the most enormous bed she'd ever seen. Covered with a feather duvet, pillows, pillows and more pillows, it was the sort of bed you could invite a small army to share.

'Is it big enough?' Matt asked, sounding anxious, and she almost choked.

'How did you get this here?' she squeaked. 'How did you even get it up the stairs?'

'Helicopters,' he told her. 'And manpower and money. Wasn't it lucky there weren't any bush fires this week?'

'Matt, this must have cost you...'

'I don't care what it cost.' He set her down carefully, tenderly on her feet. 'As long as it gets me what I want.' And then he hesitated. 'No. That's wrong. As long as it lets me be... who I am.'

'Oh, Matt.' All she wanted was for him to hold her and never let her go but somehow she had to ask. The sensible part of her was still making its unwanted presence felt. 'So, Matt, who are you?'

'I'll tell you who I am,' he said softly, lovingly, and he took her into his arms again and tugged her against his chest. 'Right this minute? I'm a man who's totally, completely, awesomely, undeniably in love with Meg O'Hara. I feel like I'm part of her and that's my biggest thing. It's what I want to be. Meg, I've asked you to marry me before, but it was different. I'm asking you again now. Meg O'Hara, the thing I want to be more than anything in the world is to be married to you. To be allowed to love you, for now and for ever. I want to *be* loved by Meg and I want to *be* allowed to love her back. So, Meg O'Hara... For the third and best time... Will you marry me?'

And how was a woman to reply to that?

There was no choice because Matt was holding her. Matt was loving her.

Her Matt.

'I guess the answer has to be yes,' she whispered.

He set her back a little. 'That sounds like you're being forced.'

'Not forced,' she whispered. 'Never forced, my love.' And then she thought, *I need to get this right. I need to say it like it is.*

'Matt, I will indeed marry you but I am being forced,' she admitted. 'Not by you, though. By me. I believe I fell in love with you the moment we met. We saved each other and we did so much more. We figured out who we are. So me... I'm the woman who loves Matt McLellan. I'm the woman who'll help you adopt Henry, who'll help care for Peggy. I'm the woman who'll egg you on to save turtles and whatever else we can save along the way. But more than that. I'm the woman who'll stay with you for ever, even if it means staying here for longer than Charlie's charter, trying out this ridiculous bed, even if we have to burn our boat again to do it. Forced? I can't deny what I am, Matt McLellan. I'm the woman who's head over heels in love with you for ever.'

And that was that. The doubts fell away. He was her man, she thought, and she was his woman. For ever and ever and ever.

And the gleam in Matt's lovely eyes said he knew it, too. Their world was starting anew.

'I have news for you,' Matt said as he gathered her into his arms again and carried her over to the preposterous bed. 'I warned Charlie that we may be quite some time. I'm not stupid. I've set up radio checks every night. I've also asked Maureen to take care of your chooks. We're stocked with human food and dog food. Apart from that…is there anything at all to stop us staying here?'

'For ever?' she breathed. 'I guess the world will break in soon enough.'

'But it'll be our world,' Matt said, and then he kissed her, tenderly, joyfully, wonderfully. 'It'll be our world for ever, my beautiful Meg. Starting now.'

* * * * *

LET'S TALK

Romance

For exclusive extracts, competitions
and special offers, find us online:

 facebook.com/millsandboon

 @millsandboonuk

 @millsandboon

Or get in touch on 0844 844 1351*

For all the latest titles coming soon,
visit millsandboon.co.uk/nextmonth

Want even more
ROMANCE?

Join our bookclub today!

'Mills & Boon books, the perfect way to escape for an hour or so.'

Miss W. Dyer

'Excellent service, promptly delivered and very good subscription choices.'

Miss A. Pearson

'You get fantastic special offers and the chance to get books before they hit the shops'

Mrs V. Hall

Visit millsandbook.co.uk/Bookclub
and save on brand new books.

MILLS & BOON